A

Holly Brannigan
MYSTERY
DONNYMEAD CASTLE

*To Katie
Happy Reading
Kathleen W. Forbes*

Kathleen W. Forbes

DONNYMEAD CASTLE
Copyright © 2015 by Kathleen W. Forbes

All rights reserved. Neither this publication nor any part of this publication may be reproduced or transmitted in any form or by any means, electronic or mechanical, including photocopying, recording or any information storage and retrieval system, without permission in writing from the author.

This is a work of fiction. Names, characters, places and incidents either are the product of the author's imagination or are used fictitiously, and any resemblance to actual persons, living or dead, businesses, companies, events, or locales is entirely coincidental.

Printed in Canada

ISBN: 978-1-4866-0801-0

Word Alive Press
131 Cordite Road, Winnipeg, MB R3W 1S1
www.wordalivepress.ca

WORD ALIVE
—PRESS—

FSC
MIX
Paper from responsible sources
FSC® C016245

Library and Archives Canada Cataloguing in Publication

Forbes, Kathleen W., 1930-, author
　　Donnymead Castle / Kathleen W. Forbes.

(A Holly Brannigan mystery)
Issued in print and electronic formats.
ISBN 978-1-4866-0801-0 (pbk.).-- SBN 978-1-4866-0802-7 (pdf).--
ISBN 978-1-4866-0803-4 (html).--ISBN 978-1-4866-0804-1 (epub)

　　I. Title II. Series: Forbes, Kathleen W., 1930- Holly Brannigan mystery.

PS8611.O7215H65 2015　　　jC813'.6　　　C2015-901534-0
　　　　　　　　　　　　　　　　　　　　　　C2015-901535-9

TABLE OF CONTENTS

1	CHAPTER 1:	*Donnymead Castle*
9	CHAPTER 2:	*The Gypsies*
22	CHAPTER 3:	*Lady Carolyn*
27	CHAPTER 4:	*The Grand Tour*
36	CHAPTER 5:	*The Cave*
46	CHAPTER 6:	*The Treasure Box*
56	CHAPTER 7:	*Sinister Undertones*
64	CHAPTER 8:	*Terror*
71	CHAPTER 9:	*The Reunion*
80	CHAPTER 10:	*The Plan*
87	CHAPTER 11:	*Guilty by Association*
90	CHAPTER 12:	*Success*
97	CHAPTER 13:	*Home Sweet Castle*
101	CHAPTER 14:	*Toast to a Lady Gypsy*

Donnymead Castle

CHAPTER 1

AS THE CAR MOVED SLOWLY UP THE HILL, HOLLY FELT THE EXCITEMENT SURGE through her. The road wound around the side of the cliff and had become very narrow. As she looked out the window to her right, her stomach felt quite uneasy, and she wondered what would happen if another car were to come down as they were going up. It was bad enough that they drove on the wrong side of the road in Ireland, which made travelling a nerve-wracking experience to say the least, but if another car were to meet them … well! She didn't dare to think about it.

The little village of Donnymead was in the valley below, and Holly thought how quaint it looked. It was more like a postcard setting than a real village. As she glanced over her right shoulder, she noticed a wooded area behind the village. It was like an aerial view, and there was a little clearing that looked like a campground of sorts. There were several trailers or wagons, and Holly could see the smoke from the campfires. The car gave a lurch, and Susan Brannigan clutched the hand strap on the back of the front seat.

"My goodness, Holly, this is worse than driving through the Rocky Mountains. At least we have good roads in Canada. If we ever reach your grandmother's house alive, I'll be a nervous wreck."

Holly silently agreed with her mother and closed her eyes as the car wound around a particularly sharp curve that didn't seem wide enough for the car. She barely heard the driver as he chatted away to her mother, assuring her that he had driven on this road hundreds of times and knew it like the back of his hand.

His name was Pat Gallagher. He had introduced himself when they got off the bus and told them that old Mrs. Brannigan had told his son, Tim, to make sure that Pat met them at the bus. Pat ran the only taxi and delivery service in the village. He also had a lorry, which Holly guessed must be a truck, so he was kept quite busy. Tim looked after deliveries from Duffy's Grocery and also handled the milk deliveries from the dairy.

Suddenly, a huge black horse galloped wildly around a curve. Pat jammed his foot on the brake. The horse reared up on its haunches, and for one sickening moment time stood still for Holly and her mother. They both watched in horror as the rider tried to quiet the animal down.

The horse pranced perilously close to the edge of the precipice. The rider must have been unaware of his peril, or he surely would have jumped to safety. After what seemed like an eternity, the young man managed to coax the trembling animal over against the inside wall of the cliff. When he had eased the horse around the car, he kicked her belly with his heels and was gone down the hillside in a flash. Pat Gallagher mopped his perspiring brow.

"Sure I thought he was a goner! That young feller looked like the devil himself was after him. I wonder who he is. Don't think I've ever seen him in these parts before. If he manages to reach the bottom without killing himself, it will be a miracle indeed."

The car started cautiously forward again and began its climb up the steepest part of the road. Susan Brannigan fanned herself nervously with her gloves. She was relieved when Pat Gallagher told her they were almost there. Holly had regained her composure and became interested again in her surroundings.

As they rounded the top of the hill, Holly gasped with delight. What a super time she would have exploring. How she wished there was someone her own age that she could share it with. Her mother had forgotten her previous terror and managed an awestruck exclamation.

"Ohhhh, it's absolutely breathtaking!"

"It is at that," said Pat Gallagher. "No matter how often I come up here, it's as though I'm seeing it for the first time."

The sea stretched out far below them, and there on the top of the hill, looking like something out of a fairy tale, majestic against the skyline, stood Donnymead Castle. It was almost surrounded by water, with steep precipices that were originally meant to guard it against invaders from the sea. The only accessible road leading into the castle was over a narrow, enclosed bridge spanning a deep chasm. No wonder her grandmother had refused to leave when her grandpa had died. Holly and her mother had been unable to come for the funeral, as Holly had been ill. Her father had come alone and had tried to persuade her grandmother to come back with him to Canada, but to no avail.

Grandma was standing by the big iron gate when they drove up. She had just started to worry about them, as they were overdue. She lived in the gatekeeper's cottage. It had been her home for forty-two years.

Charlie, her husband, had helped old Tom McClure take care of the grounds and keep vandals off the place, but when he died last year, she had refused to move. She liked it here, and here she would stay.

She ran to meet them; her arms stretched wide, the tears of joy streaming down her face.

Laughing and crying all at the same time, she hugged them both, and then held Holly out so she could look at her.

"Oh, Pat! Will you just look at her! Have you ever seen a face like that? We won't be able to keep the boys away."

"Aye," said Pat. "There isn't a colleen in the village that could hold a candle to her beauty. Takes after her mother and grandmother she does."

"Hold your tongue now, Pat. Too much blarney won't be good for Holly on her first day here. I've got the kettle on, so let's go inside. You too, Pat, and we'll have a cup of tea before you start back."

"The tea sounds wonderful, Mother Brannigan," said Susan. "I need something to settle my nerves. We just had the most harrowing experience."

"You don't say? Oh, I suppose you mean the road up here." Grandma was nodding her head as she spoke. "Yes, it does shake a body up a mite the first trip, but you get used to it after a while."

"Oh, I don't think that's what Mrs. Brannigan meant," Pat explained. "We almost had a bit of an accident on the last curve back there."

Grandma Brannigan's hands flew to her face.

"Bless me soul, Pat! What do you mean?"

"Well now," said Pat. "Did you happen to notice a young feller on a horse tearing down the road like a wild man?"

"As a matter of fact, I wondered who that was. So tell me what happened now."

"Well," Pat continued, "he almost ran smack into us. It's a miracle he wasn't thrown over the edge. I'm afraid he put a scare into the ladies. I tell you, I was sittin' on the edge of the seat meself. It's one experience I've no wish to repeat, and I intend to make it my business to find out who that rascal is and give him a piece of me mind."

Grandma Brannigan poured the tea and agreed that the man needed to be told. Holly was wishing they would hurry and finish tea so she could unpack some of her things and change into something more suitable for exploring. She had so many questions to ask her grandmother about the castle. She wondered if anyone lived there, and she had noticed smoke coming out of the chimney of the little cottage behind the castle. It seemed out of place in such a setting.

Suddenly, Holly realized that Pat Gallagher was speaking to her. He was getting ready to leave and was telling her that Tim would be out in the morning with the milk and groceries, and he was sure his son would be more than happy to show Holly around. He said Tim knew the cliffs and the woods better than anybody, and could acquaint her with the history of the castle and village and show her the points of interest.

Holly thanked him and said she would be looking forward to meeting Tim. Her mother also thanked him. He said goodbye, taking the grocery list that Grandmother had prepared. Grandma Brannigan bustled about, showing them through the cottage. It was larger than it looked from the outside. There were two bedrooms downstairs, a parlour, a lovely big kitchen, and a small bathroom.

Holly was surprised that there was a plumbing system in such a remote area and said so. Her grandmother explained that it was a rather crude system with a septic tank and pump that was powered by the same generator that produced the electricity. While water was being used, the pump could be heard quite distinctly somewhere in the cellar. Grandma demonstrated as she spoke and said she didn't quite understand it, she only knew that it worked. Pat Gallagher and Tom McClure serviced it twice a year.

Holly inquired if there was plumbing in the castle, and was told that Lord Mead had put the same system in the west wing some forty years ago. The system was often in need of servicing. The castle now belonged to Lord Mead's nephew, Sir Robert Mead. He inherited the estate on the death of his uncle, as he was the only known surviving relative.

Lord Mead had been very generous to Holly's grandparents and Tom McClure and his wife in his bequests to them. They all received a pension for life and five thousand pounds each, along with letters commending them on their long and trustworthy service. The cottages were to be their homes as long as they lived.

Holly asked if anyone lived in the castle at the present time and was told that Sir Robert had boarded most of it up and closed off all but a small suite of eighteen rooms in the west wing, which Tom McClure and his wife always kept in readiness. Sir Robert used the castle as a retreat and did not always inform them in advance of his intention to arrive. Some areas of the castle were badly in need of repair.

Sir Robert maintained several large estates and used the castle only once or twice a year. His business interests took him all over the world. He spent two months of the year in the Mediterranean, several months in America, and part of the year in Switzerland, where he owned a chalet.

What a shame to own such a wonderful, historical old castle and to lock it up, seldom to enjoy it. Holly knew her imagination would run wild if she ever spent one night in it. She knew that in all probability this would never happen, but dreaming is all part of living, and if one has imagination, it can be very interesting at times.

She was delighted with her bedroom. It was the only room upstairs and was a converted attic. Everywhere she looked there were ruffles and lace, and there was a rocking chair beside the fireplace. That was something else Holly had noticed. There were fireplaces in every room in the cottage. When she commented on this, her grandmother explained that there was no central heating in Ireland and that was why there was a fireplace in every room. *What a wonderful idea*, thought Holly. This was much cozier that central heating. The firelight made everything glow, and the burning peat had a strange, pleasing aroma.

Enough daydreaming! It was ten minutes past six when Holly had unpacked and put her clothes away. She hadn't meant to do it all until evening, but she couldn't find her sneakers, and wouldn't you know it, there they were in the very last bag, right at the bottom. *Oh well ... at least a rather unpleasant job was finished*, she thought as she closed the last bag and put it in the back of the closet. A girl just couldn't go exploring without her sneakers. She tied her laces and ran down the stairs two at a time, kissed her mother and grandmother, and told them she was going to look around before dark.

"Well, be careful, now," her grandmother warned. "The cliffs are dangerous."

"Don't worry," Holly assured her. "I just want to get a closer look at the castle."

"Off you go then, dear. Sir Robert isn't here at this time of the year, so it will be alright for you to explore."

The air was brisk and Holly took deep breaths as she headed toward the little bridge. She was intrigued by the shed that covered the bridge. It seemed out of place and looked as though it had been built quite recently. She must remember to ask Tim about it tomorrow, as she didn't want to keep pestering her grandmother with questions. She had to admit to herself that she was thankful the bridge was covered, as her quick look into the chasm left her slightly dizzy.

Running quickly across the bridge, Holly blinked several times as she felt the shadows and light hit her face. All at once she had left the present behind, and the atmosphere of fifteenth century Ireland had engulfed her. She looked down at her clothes and dismissed them with her mind, seeing herself instead in a high buttoned flowing gown with a mantilla on her head, held high at the crown with some sort of rigid frame.

At the same moment, her bearing became more ladylike, straight and tall, her head held high, as she walked along the lane that bordered the west wing of the castle. Holly stopped to admire an old sundial. She had seen one like it in a museum once. It was covered with ivy, as were the walls of the castle, but great pains had been taken to keep the face of the sundial clean, and the ivy had been trimmed neatly around it.

Holly had been so engrossed in her thoughts that a sudden movement behind her startled her out of her reverie. Turning quickly, she realized that she was the object of some amusement. The lady was old, possibly seventy or more. Her shining white hair was pulled up in a proud bun, and her brown silk dress flowed to her ankles. Her head was cocked slightly to one side, and Holly hoped that she was friendly.

"Sorry to have startled you, my dear. I am Cora McClure, and you must be Holly, Mary's granddaughter."

"How do you do," Holly managed and hoped she had said the proper thing. Somehow she didn't think a simple "hello" would have been quite appropriate. Mrs. McClure had a certain presence about her that lent itself to the past and commanded a proper greeting; however, she did seem friendly enough.

"I hope you don't mind," Holly said apologetically. "Grandmother said it would be alright if I looked around."

"Of course you may. Drop in to my cottage tomorrow afternoon and I'll have tea and cakes ready. I know how curious you must be about the castle, and I can tell you things about it that nobody else can."

"Thank you very much, Mrs. McClure, but Tim Gallagher is coming tomorrow to help me explore."

"Tim's a nice boy," she said. "Not too many nice boys these days. Tom would enjoy Tim's company, so bring him with you for tea. I'll promise you a story or two that even Tim hasn't heard before."

The old lady's eyes danced and Holly assured her they would be there around three.

"Good! I'll expect you then, and perhaps I can persuade Tom to take you both on a tour through the castle. He's always in a good mood after tea and cakes."

"Oh, super!" Holly exclaimed with delight. She had forgotten her earlier decision to say just the right thing.

"I can't wait to tell Mom and Grandma the news," she went on. "See you tomorrow, Mrs. McClure, and thanks again."

Holly was in such a hurry to tell her mother of her good fortune in being offered a tour of the castle that she paused only briefly for one last, quick look at the ivy covered walls and towers.

Cora McClure smiled as she watched Holly, her feet barely touching the ground as she flew like the wind toward the bridge. Gone was the regal bearing, the play acting that she had witnessed when she had caught Holly off guard at the sundial. Was it so long ago? Almost forty years. A lot had happened since then. Yes, she had stories to tell. When she had been standing at the sundial, Holly had borne such a resemblance to Lady Carolyn that it had been quite startling, and Cora McClure was lost in reverie as she recalled the past.

The Gypsies

CHAPTER 2

HER GRANDMA HAD SURE BEEN SURPRISED WHEN HOLLY BURST IN WITH HER news last night. She said she couldn't remember the last time Cora McClure had made such an offer.

"They usually send anyone packing who even comes near the castle," was her puzzled comment.

Holly wasn't about to question her good fortune, however, and this morning she was up and dressed by eight o'clock, which was, to say the least, unusual, since she was, after all, on her holidays. Her grandma had heard her and had her breakfast on the table when she came downstairs. What a breakfast! Homemade muffins, sausages and eggs, with hot potato bread smothered in butter, and tea.

Her father liked his coffee in the morning, and she wondered how he would take to tea for breakfast. He was unable to come with Holly and her mother, as something unexpected had detained him in his job as a lawyer for one of the largest firms in Vancouver. He said he would follow them in a week at the latest.

Grandma had been a little disappointed, but was glad that they had come on ahead. Her mom came into the kitchen just as Holly finished her breakfast.

"Hi, Mom," she grinned, her hands over her stomach. "Wait till you see what Grandma has done to my figure. We're both going to get fat!"

Grandma laughed. "It wouldn't hurt either one of you if you added another ten pounds or so."

"Heaven forbid!" Her mother pretended to be horrified at the thought.

Holly had just finished helping her grandmother with the dishes when she heard something outside. There was a knock at the door, and a tall, good-looking boy about Holly's age came in, his arms full of groceries.

"Ah! Now Tim, you're just in time. I'd like to have you meet my granddaughter and her mother. Holly and Susan, this is Pat's son, Tim. Put the groceries over there, Tim, and come and welcome them."

Tim greeted them both and asked Holly if she would like to go with him on the rest of his milk rounds.

"There's plenty of room on the cart, and I'll have you back in time for lunch," he coaxed her. "Then I'll take the afternoon off and show you the sights."

Holly didn't have to be coaxed. She liked Tim immediately, and told him about their invitation to tea and cakes and their promised tour of the castle.

"Wow! That's a piece of luck. Mrs. McClure must have taken a fancy to you, Holly. Don't worry; we'll be back in plenty of time. We can't turn down a chance like that. Isn't that a corker, Mrs. Brannigan?" He shook his head, puzzled. "And a tour of the castle as well?"

"That's what I told them," Mrs. Brannigan agreed. "It sure is strange indeed."

Tim helped Holly onto the cart and they waved goodbye to her mother and grandmother. Just as the horse started off, someone called out.

"Hold on a minute, Tim. The Missus wants some milk and cream. Hope you have some extra."

A tall, grey haired man was hurrying out of the bridge shed. His face was rugged and lined, but he moved fast, like an animal, which was surprising for a man of his obvious years. Holly guessed that this must be Tom McClure.

"Good mornin' to you, Mr. McClure. If I'd known you wanted something, I'd have brought it in to you."

Tim obviously liked the old man, for he hurried to serve him.

"Well now, Tim, I understand we're having some very special visitors this afternoon, and Cora needs some nice, thick cream for whipping. She's baking some fancy cakes for the occasion, so don't be late, young fellow," he admonished him. "And this must be the young lady I've been hearing about. The Missus was right. She is a beauty indeed."

"This is Holly Brannigan, Mr. McClure," Tim introduced them.

"A pleasure to meet you, young lady, I hope we'll all make your visit one to remember. Take good care of her now, Tim," he cautioned as he paid for his purchases. Then with a wave he went over to the cottage to exchange pleasantries with Holly's mother and grandmother.

What super friendly people the Irish were! Holly loved the way they talked in a pleasant, rolling brogue, and they were so polite. At least those she had met so far certainly were.

The horse moved at an easy gait down the road, and Tim asked her about Canada and said he hoped to go there someday. He said he had an uncle in Toronto and wondered if that was far from Vancouver, where Holly lived. Holly said it was almost as far from Vancouver to Toronto as it was from Vancouver to Ireland. It took some time for Tim to digest this news and to realize the vastness of Canada. He had been about to ask if she knew his uncle, but now he realized how ridiculous this question would be.

The trip into the village was quite uneventful. Perhaps, as her grandmother had said, she was getting used to the road. She had noticed some small boats on the water and told Tim they reminded her of home, as her father had a small sailboat that he kept at Lion's Bay.

"MY POP HAS A LITTLE ROW BOAT," SAID TIM. "I'LL TAKE YOU OUT IN IT TOMORROW if you like and show you the cave."

"Super!" exclaimed Holly. "Oh, I know I'm going to love it here. I've never been in a cave before."

As they drove into the village, a small, ragged boy about twelve years old darted out of Duffy's store and into an alley. A short, tubby little man wearing an apron charged out of the store waving a meat cleaver and yelling at the top of his lungs.

"Stop, ye little thief! Come back here at once or I'll boil yer hide for breakfast" ... a threat that only resulted in urging the boy to run faster.

Tim jumped off the cart and ran after the culprit.

"That's it, Tim me boy, go get him," he yelled. "These thievin' gypsies are robbin' me blind."

Tim followed the boy down the alley and through the back yards of the next street. The boy jumped over a style and streaked across a field in the direction of the woods. Tim knew he wouldn't be able to catch him before he reached the woods, so he decided to go back and finish his rounds.

"I'll finish my deliveries, Mr. Duffy, and then I'll look for him. By that time, he'll think we have stopped looking for him, and he'll probably be back at the camp. What did he steal, anyway?"

"I was wrappin' a chicken for Mrs. McCarthy and turned my back for just a second to get the tape, and the young scallywag grabbed the parcel and took off like a rabbit."

"Well, I doubt if we'll find your chicken, but maybe we'll find your thief. What do you want me to do with him if I do find him?"

"Just bring him here, and we'll let Constable Millar decide that. The boy needs a lesson."

In all the confusion, Mr. Duffy hadn't noticed Holly, who was still sitting on the cart. He was turning to go back into the shop when he suddenly realized that here was a prospective customer whom he had completely ignored.

"Ah, Tim, me lad, haven't ye forgotten something?" He was studying Holly with obvious approval.

"Oh, I'm sorry, Mr. Duffy. This is Mrs. Brannigan's granddaughter, Holly. She's visiting from Canada."

"Welcome to Donnymead, Miss Holly. Sorry you had to witness such goings on. Are you planning to stay long?"

"Just six weeks, Mr. Duffy. We have to be home at the end of August to get ready for school."

"Anybody as pretty as you are doesn't need brains," said Mr. Duffy. "What are you planning to do when you finish school, Holly?"

"I hope to be a lawyer, but of course that is a long way off. I have many years of schooling to look forward to."

"Well, in that case, the brains are necessary. You certainly have high aspirations, and I wish you luck. Our little gypsy thief could do with a lesson in the law. Perhaps he'll be your first client!"

Mr. Duffy was teasing, of course, but Holly wondered why the boy found it necessary to steal food. Was he hungry? Were his parents unable to provide for him, or did he in fact have parents? Then again, perhaps he had been taught to steal.

Holly asked Tim if he would take her with him when he went in search of the boy. She said she was curious about the gypsies' way of life and wondered if the boy's thieving was perhaps prompted by hunger. She found it curious that he would steal food and not just candy or something more interesting to a small boy.

"Listen to that now," said Mr. Duffy. "She already sounds like a lawyer. Run along both of you, or you'll have me feeling sorry for the little scamp."

Tim introduced Holly to several of his customers, and she was asked to drop in for tea at the McCarthy's and Sullivan's. She wondered if people were friendly in all small towns, or if Donnymead was an exception. It certainly wasn't so in the city.

As they were on their way back to Mr. Duffy's store to drop off the empty bottles and ice that was used to refrigerate the milk, cream, and butter, Holly caught a glimpse of the young man who had very nearly met his doom the previous day on the cliffs of Castle Road. He was riding the beautiful, black horse and was headed in the direction of the woods. Holly pointed him out to Tim and told him of yesterday's traumatic experience.

"Oh yes," said Tim, "I heard Pop telling Ma about it last night. Can't say that I know him, though. He's a stranger around here, and he's too well dressed to be one of the gypsies. Maybe Mr. Duffy knows who he is."

Mr. Duffy didn't, though he, too, had seen him on several occasions, but always on the horse. He would find out about him if the man came into the store, as Mr. Duffy had a natural curiosity and inquiring mind where his customers were concerned, and there wasn't much he couldn't find out about them. Since his was the only grocery store in the village, everyone eventually showed up there, so he had no doubt but that the stranger would become one of his customers.

Tim emptied the cart and proceeded in the direction of the woods in search of the chicken thief. The caravan tracks were easy to follow, as it had been raining on the afternoon two days ago when the gypsies had sought shelter in the woods and had set up camp. The horse ambled along slowly while Holly and Tim asked each other questions about their respective lifestyles, schooling, and friends.

Tim told Holly that he was sixteen and a half, and Holly said that she would be sixteen next week, on Tuesday, July 25th. Her father promised her he would be here for her birthday, and she asked Tim if he would come to her grandma's to help her celebrate. Her grandma had promised her a special cake and other goodies, and Holly wanted Tim to meet her father.

"Of course I'll come, Holly. I wouldn't miss it for the world. Whoa! There boy!" yelled Tim, as he pulled on the reins.

They had found the clearing. Three caravans and six tents were scattered in no apparent order around a large campfire over which the contents of several pots were cooking. The aroma that assailed their nostrils left little doubt about the inevitable destination of the chicken, or so it would seem.

A gypsy woman and a girl about thirteen or fourteen years old were tending the pots. Several women were in the process of making baskets, and a couple of men were occupied in the art of saddle making. The black horse that the mysterious young man had been riding was grazing close by along with several others, but the man who rode it was nowhere in sight.

The gypsies showed only slight interest in Holly and Tim and kept on with what they were doing. The women all wore bright coloured kerchiefs on their heads, large earrings, and long, gaily coloured dresses.

THERE WAS NO SIGN OF THE BOY WHO STOLE THE CHICKEN, ALTHOUGH SEVEN or eight children were in plain view. Three of them were playing with a ball, while two were having target practice with a couple of sling shots. None of them, however, appeared neglected like the boy who stole the chicken.

Tim climbed down off the cart, and Holly followed him. He had started toward one of the men when the door of the largest caravan opened, and the man who had been riding the horse came down the steps and walked toward them. He was tall, dark, and very handsome with eyes black as coal, and he took charge of the situation immediately.

"Can I help you?" he asked as he eyed them suspiciously.

He didn't look like a gypsy, and his inquiry had a note of arrogance about it.

"I hope so," said Tim. "Do you have a young boy here about twelve years old?" He hastened to describe him to the man.

"We don't have anyone who fits that description. As you can see, none of our people wear tattered clothes. What has he done?"

"My name is Tim Gallagher, Sir. I work for Mr. Duffy, who owns the grocery store. The boy stole a chicken from the store and ran into the woods. We naturally believed he headed for your camp," Tim explained, then turned beet red, as he realized he had said the wrong thing.

"And of course everyone assumed the boy was a gypsy," the man said coldly. "My people do not steal. We are trades people and make our living by selling the items we make. The women also tell fortunes for a price, but none of our people has ever found it necessary to steal in order to survive."

"I'm very sorry, Sir. I shouldn't have said what I did. Please accept my apology," Tim said awkwardly.

"Very well. Just remember," the man said, "things are not always as they seem."

"Sounds like a philosopher," thought Holly. The idea of having her fortune told appealed to her.

"Could I have my fortune told, please?" Holly begged excitedly. "My name is Holly Brannigan. I'm visiting here from Canada, and I've never had my fortune told before. I'll pay for it, of course."

"Bring the young lady here, Anthony." A lady had appeared at the caravan door. She apparently had overheard Holly's request.

Holly was more bewildered than ever. The lady didn't appear any more like a gypsy than the young man did. Perhaps Holly had been misinformed about how a gypsy dressed and behaved.

The lady had glorious silver hair that she wore in an upward sweep. Her black dress was long, and although it was plain, it looked elegant. Holly guessed her age to be somewhere in the fifties. She smiled warmly as she beckoned to Holly.

"Very well, Mother." The young man seemed reluctant. "Come this way," he said to Holly. "My mother will tell your fortune."

Holly followed him into the caravan. His mother indicated which chair she wished Holly to use. Holly couldn't believe her eyes. The inside of the caravan was luxurious.

It was larger than it seemed from the outside and was divided into a bedroom and living room with a little kitchen. There were laces and silks covering the furniture, and the drapes were brocade. Expensive rugs adorned the floors. Holly was quick to realize that this was not a typical gypsy caravan and commented on how beautiful it was.

"THANK YOU, MY DEAR," THE LADY SAID SOFTLY. "MY HUSBAND WAS THE SON OF the king of the gypsies. He made my life and that of our son, Anthony, very comfortable. Now my dear, I heard you tell Anthony you wanted your fortune told. You just cross my palm with silver for luck." She held her hand out as she spoke.

Holly took two pounds in silver coins out of her purse and put them in the gypsy lady's hand.

"I heard you tell my son your name was Holly Brannigan and that you were visiting here. From your speech, I would guess you to be American or Canadian. Am I right?"

"That's right," said Holly. "I'm from Canada. I'm visiting my grandmother. She lives in the gatekeeper's cottage at the castle."

"Let me look into the crystal ball, and I'll tell you what I see."

The gypsy's hands were cupped around the crystal ball, and she gazed intently into it as she spoke.

"I see a castle and two small houses close by. I see you walking through many rooms with a tall, older man and a young boy. One room is kept locked. It belonged to a young lady. There is a box behind a loose stone in the fireplace. It contains many secrets. I see a warning to be careful on the cliffs and in the cave. Someone is going to get hurt. I see long dark tunnels and danger in relation to water. There will be a discovery of great importance. The police will be involved. You will have many surprises in the next week."

It was obvious the fortune telling was over. Holly thought it was super and that she had foreseen the tour of the castle, and she told the gypsy lady that it had already been promised to her. She thanked the gypsy and her son and then told him that she had seen him the previous day on the castle road, explaining that she and her mother had been in the car that he had almost collided with.

Sudden emotion changed the expression on his face. It was apparent Holly had said something to really upset him. The colour had drained from his rich olive complexion, which was now ashen white. He was overcome with fury, and as Holly considered what could have led up to his obvious display of distress, she realized he hadn't wanted his mother to know of his near accident.

"I'm sorry," said Holly. "I guess I put my foot in my mouth."

"My son sometimes tries to spare my feelings by hiding such things from me," laughed his mother. "I'm not really as delicate as you like to think, Anthony. Now, let's not keep that young man you came with waiting any longer, Holly. If he has any preconceived ideas about gypsies, he may think we have kidnapped you. Come back and see me again," she invited her. "I would like to know how you enjoy your tour of the castle."

"Thank you, Ma'am. Oh, I don't even know your name. I'd rather not call you 'ma'am.'"

"My name is Mrs. Allegro, and I'm very pleased that you came," she said softly.

Holly said goodbye and went in search of Tim. She found him talking to one of the men, admiring his handiwork, which was a beautiful riding saddle. Holly told the gypsy that if they were still here in a week, she would bring her father to see his work and perhaps he would have a sale.

Holly noticed that when he thanked her, the gypsy had a thick foreign accent, while Mrs. Allegro and her son spoke perfect English.

"The princess loves this part of the country," he said, "so we may be here for some time."

"THE PRINCESS?" HOLLY EXCLAIMED, "OH, YOU MEAN MRS. ALLEGRO?"

"Yes," he nodded. "Did she not tell you? She is a gypsy princess."

"Oh, of course," Holly exclaimed, "she told me her husband was a son of the king of the gypsies. Then her son would also be a prince!"

"Yes, Miss!"

The gypsy continued working on the saddle as he spoke.

"I thought there was something different about them both," Holly murmured.

"Thank you for your information," said Tim. "We'd better go, Holly, as it's getting on to twelve o'clock. I expected to have you home by this time. You're going to be late for lunch."

On the way home, Tim told Holly that the gypsy had told him of seeing the young boy in the woods and that he seemed to be alone. They had been mistaken in thinking that the chicken was cooking in one of the pots, as it was rabbit stew. It was unlikely that they would find the boy if he was by himself. He'd probably gone deeper into the woods.

They had decided to drop the hunt for now when suddenly Holly started sniffing.

"I smell chicken again, Tim."

"I do too," said Tim as he jumped down off the cart. "This way, Holly, let's check it out."

Holly jumped down and followed Tim through the deep brush. Tim signaled with his finger to his lips that they must be quiet. Suddenly, they came on a clearing and saw the scrawny, undernourished boy sitting by the campfire. He had rigged up a sort of spit on which the chicken was skewered.

Holly and Tim surprised him, as he had almost fallen asleep while waiting for the chicken to cook. He jumped up in alarm, not knowing which way to run. Tim grabbed him while he was still confused and was suddenly sorry for the boy. He was nothing but skin and bones. It was obvious the boy was hungry, and he was scared to death, like a cornered animal.

"What's your name, boy?" Tim asked.

The boy cowered with his arms up over his head, as though expecting Tim to strike him.

"Don't hit me! Don't hit me!" he pleaded.

"I won't hit you," said Tim. "What's your name now?"

"Casey Donnelly, Sir."

It struck Holly and Tim as funny that the boy had called Tim "Sir," but they resisted the temptation to laugh, and only their eyes betrayed their amusement.

"Where are your parents, and why aren't they taking care of you?" asked Tim.

"They're both dead, Sir." The boy's eyes filled with tears at the mention of his parents. "Pa was taken last year, and Ma two months ago. I' bin on the road since Ma died, headin' for me Aunt Bessie's."

"Where does your Aunt Bessie live?" Holly inquired.

"She lives in Portadown, Miss, in County Armagh. It's a fur bit when yer walkin'."

He looked at them both fearfully.

"Are ye going to put me in gaol for stealin'?"

His eyes looked old and he slumped like an old man.

"How old are you, Casey?" asked Holly.

"Fourteen, Miss," he replied.

He was so pitifully small; it was hard to believe he was more that eleven or twelve.

"Mr. Duffy will have to decide what to do with you." Tim broke off a leg of the chicken as he talked and handed it to Casey.

"In the meantime, Casey, you'd better eat this. Get on the cart, and we'll get going. Mr. Duffy is not a hard man. He doesn't hold with stealing, but I think you'll find him fair."

Tim made sure that Casey was between Holly and himself on the cart to prevent his making a run for it again. Holly hoped that Mr. Duffy would not be too hard on Casey. She herself had never known hardship and wondered if she would have resorted to stealing under similar circumstances. The boy ate the chicken leg like he hadn't had a meal for a week. She wondered when he had eaten last. He looked so frightened.

It was five minutes after one when Tim pulled up in front of Duffy's store. Mr. Duffy came out, wiping his hands on his apron. When he saw the boy, his eyes lit up, and he pointed an accusing finger.

"Tim, me boy, I see you found him. Get the young rascal down here. These gypsies are going to learn they can't steal from Joseph P. Duffy and get away with it."

The boy had shrunk to half his size in fear and started to cry. Tim told Mr. Duffy what he had discovered and explained that he was not one of the gypsies. As Tim talked, Mr. Duffy's face softened, and his eyes took in the wretched little frame of the boy. He was ashamed he hadn't noticed at first how pathetically thin and small he was, and his heart went out to the boy.

"Leave him to me, Tim. Come on, Casey. The first thing we're going to do is feed you. Then we'll see what we can do about finding your Aunt Bessie."

Casey was wiping his eyes with his hands and looking at Mr. Duffy as though he couldn't believe his ears. Tim winked at Holly as he said to Mr. Duffy, "I always knew you were soft hearted, Mr. Duffy."

"Well, don't tell my customers," he said gruffly, "or they'll think I'm soft in the head as well, and one of these days, I won't have a business."

When Holly and Tim left them, Mr. Duffy eased Casey's mind somewhat with his show of concern for the boy. He took Casey through his store and into his apartment, patting his shoulders to show he was safe, and wondering what he would tell Mrs. Duffy.

Holly realized her grandma and mom would be wondering what had happened to her, but she had lots to tell them, and she knew they would understand. Tim was urging the horse to a trot as it was now twenty past two, and they were due at the McClure's at three o'clock. The time had gone so fast today, and Holly wondered if the rest of her holiday would be as interesting.

The tide was out, and Holly noticed that the entrance to the cave was completely visible. This morning it had been partially covered by water. She pointed this out to Tim.

"You're very observant, Holly," he replied. "The tides here are very unpredictable, but I'm afraid we'll have to put our exploring of the cave off till tomorrow, as we have a pretty full day planned so far. We wasted a lot of time in the woods today, although I suppose, in a way, it wasn't wasted."

Holly agreed that the time hadn't been wasted and told Tim she'd had a wonderful time, and was grateful that Casey had been found. She knew that Mr. Duffy would do what he could to help him.

They arrived at Holly's grandmother's with only twenty-five minutes to spare before they were expected at Mr. and Mrs. McClure's. She kissed her mom and grandma and asked Tim to explain why they were late as she ran off to change into something more suitable for visiting. Her choice was a black skirt and white silk blouse.

She wanted to make a good impression and didn't think her jeans were appropriate. When she came downstairs, she saw that her mother and grandma were listening intently to Tim's account of their morning. Her grandma was especially interested in the gypsy woman and her son, and Holly told her of the unusual encounter.

"You'd better both run along now," Susan Brannigan reminded them, "or you'll be late at the McClure's."

Holly glanced at her watch.

"We'd better go, Tim. It's three o'clock."

They hurried out of the house and ran in the direction of Cora and Tom McClure's.

Lady Carolyn

CHAPTER 3

CORA MCCLURE WATCHED HOLLY AND TIM HURRYING AROUND THE WALK AND then called to Tom.

"Here they come, Tom. You realize it's been almost ten years since we've had young people in the house?"

She was looking forward to the visit and went to the door to greet her young callers. When Holly and Tim arrived, she was standing at the door waiting to welcome them.

"How nice to see you again, Holly and Tim."

"I hope we're not late, Mrs. McClure," Holly said.

"Not at all, my dear. You're very punctual." She put her arm around Holly. "Come on in and tell us what you've been doing. I hope Tim has been making your day interesting so far."

"I've been doing my best, Mrs. McClure," said Tim. "We've had quite an unusual morning."

Cora McClure led them into a cozy little parlour. Her husband, Tom, was stoking the fire and greeted them with a cheery wave.

"Come and sit by the fire," he invited them. "Did I hear you say you had an unusual morning? What could you discover in Donnymead that would make your morning unusual?"

Once they were seated, Holly and Tim told of their visit with the gypsies and of the young boy they had found in the woods. The McClure's listened with obvious interest, and were especially interested in the young gypsy named Anthony. They had seen him the previous day and had noted his apparent interest in the castle. Both of them commented that he didn't look like the average run-of-the-mill gypsy, and Holly proceeded to tell them of his mother and her unusual living quarters. Her story included an account of the gypsy's predictions with regard to the tour of the castle, the secret locked room, and the tunnels, as well as her warning that someone would be hurt.

During the account of the morning's happenings, Mrs. McClure had been busy pouring the tea, and now and then at certain points in their story she would stare into space and say, "I wonder if it's possible."

Tom gave her a strange, inquiring look that wasn't missed by Holly or Tim. The old lady had a faraway look in her eyes, and as she handed Holly and Tim their teas, she muttered something about the past always coming back to haunt a body.

"Why, whatever do you mean, Mrs. McClure?" Holly was all ears now.

"Have some of these cakes that I baked especially for you," she coaxed them. "They're called jelly flans."

Holly took one of the little sponge cakes with jelly filling and topped with luscious whipped cream. The cakes were passed around and then Cora McClure sat down with her tea on her lap.

"I promised you a story, Holly. There are many stories about the castle, some fact and some fiction. Your unusual account of this morning brought to mind something that happened many years ago."

Mrs. McClure was staring into space, and it was obvious that her mind had wandered back over the span of time to another era and things that were long forgotten except by her. She paused for a few moments to gather her thoughts, and then she told them an incredible story.

"I came to work for Lord and Lady Mead fifty nine years ago when I was a young girl of eighteen. Lord and Lady Mead had two children: Master William, who was five years old, and Lady Carolyn, the new baby. I was the children's nanny and was given complete charge of the nursery. The children were my life in those days. The castle was a very busy place. Lord and Lady Mead did a lot of entertaining. There were elegant carriages coming and going and fancy new automobiles they called roadsters. England was at war with Germany, and the world had gone mad."

Tim and Holly were so intent on what Mrs. McClure was saying that the tea was forgotten, and the little cakes had lost their appeal. Their eyes were riveted on Cora McClure while she took them back through the most colourful period of her life.

"Lord Mead owned a wonderful string of horses in those days, and often they had fox hunts in the woods and meadows. Lady Carolyn and Master William learned to ride when they were only toddlers, and I worried as though they were my own every time they got on a horse. When they were in their teens, they would ride into the woods together, even though they had been told by Lord and Lady Mead never to go alone."

There was another momentary pause, and nobody else moved or spoke. Mrs. McClure was leaning back in her rocking chair, and her eyes were half closed as she went on.

"They often came home and told me of the gypsy camps in the woods. I was always afraid that they would get into trouble on one of these foolhardy trips, but they wouldn't listen to my pleas. One day when Sir William was twenty one years old, they went riding as usual. This time Sir William was carried home by the gypsies. He was dead. He had ridden like the wind, Lady Carolyn told us, and a low hanging branch knocked him off his horse. He had been looking over his shoulder at Lady Carolyn and hadn't noticed the branch. His neck was broken, and he died instantly. That young man on the horse yesterday reminded me of him, so wild and reckless he was."

Cora dabbed her eyes with a handkerchief, wiping an imaginary tear as she recalled this traumatic event.

"Lady Carolyn was inconsolable, and often she rode into the woods by herself in spite of her parents' warnings. Tom and I lived in this little cottage at that time. We were married when I was past thirty, and though my position as nanny was about over, there was plenty to keep me busy on Lady Mead's personal staff. Tom trained and cared for the horses. Lady Carolyn came home one day after one of her rides in the woods, and she told me she had a secret. She said she was in love with a prince, but I mustn't tell anyone. I was amused, but I promised I wouldn't tell a soul."

The suspicion of a smile played around her mouth as Cora related this treasure of memorabilia.

"The following month, Lady Carolyn was sent to a private school in England, though she protested that she didn't want to go. She was seventeen at the time, and her parents thought it was time for her to become a polished young lady. She cried the whole week before she left and spent many hours in the woods. By the time she was ready to leave, a strange serenity had come over her, and she seemed resigned to her parents' decision. Six weeks after she began her schooling, Lady Carolyn disappeared and was never heard of again. Lord Mead employed investigators all over the world in an effort to trace her, but the search proved fruitless. It was believed that she had met with foul play."

Tom McClure leaned forward and put some peat on the fire, and as it crackled into flame, the effect was hypnotic. Cora went on.

"Lady Mead pined for her daughter and took to her bed, where she remained until she died. Your grandmother came to work for Lady Mead at this time, Holly, as Lady Mead was in need of constant care. She never left her bedroom suite in twenty eight years. Lord Mead also became withdrawn and no longer entertained. The horses were sold, and Tom and your grandfather took care of the grounds. All but the west wing of the castle was closed off, and the staff was dismissed except for two maids, a cook, three cleaning staff, your grandparents, Tom, and me. Lady Carolyn's room is still exactly as it was when she left forty years ago. Lord Mead said it was to be kept locked, but I have a key, and I go in periodically and keep the dust away. I always hoped that someday she would return to her home."

Cora McClure's eyes were misty, and Holly was suddenly aware that her tea was cold and she had forgotten all about her delicious cake. She had relived almost sixty years with Mrs. McClure and could feel the sadness of the other's loss. Tim was unusually quiet, and then he told them that the people in the village never really knew what the true story was about Lady Carolyn, and there were many stories going around, even one about a ghost and strange lights at night.

They had some more tea and cakes, and then Tom said it was time to show them the castle. He went into another room and came back with three large rings of keys. Mrs. McClure said she would come along, as she wanted to show them Lady Carolyn's room. She said she had a special reason for wanting to show it to Holly.

The Grand Tour

CHAPTER 4

THE HUGE DOUBLE OAK DOORS SWUNG INWARD, AND AGAIN HOLLY STEPPED into the past as the small procession proceeded into the great hall. The domed ceiling towered majestically above the rich panelled walls of elegantly carved oak. There were many rooms leading off each side of the hall, but the focal point was a monumental marble staircase that must have been fifteen feet wide.

The staircase was richly carpeted and wound invitingly upward to a second floor balcony. The rails were solid carved oak. There were huge carved marble pillars and statues everywhere Holly looked. She was glad she wasn't wearing her jeans as she gazed at the awe inspiring sight. It reminded her of the way she felt when she walked into church.

"I'll show you the suite that Sir Robert uses, and then we'll look at some of the rest of it," said Tom. "There are parts of the castle I haven't been in for a couple of years. It's too large to take you through in an afternoon, but I'll show you the parts that have been lived in most recently and some of the old areas."

"How many rooms are there?" Holly inquired.

"Two hundred and twenty," Tom replied, "including the ballroom. Of course, there are the wine cellars and the dungeons down below, but the dungeons haven't been used in over a hundred years."

Tom had ushered them into a spacious parlour as he spoke. There was a gigantic fireplace along one wall. Another wall boasted many tall, frosted windows that were adorned with heavy, wine velvet drapes. The other walls held huge paintings in beautifully carved frames. The furniture was covered with dust throws, but Holly could see that the room was elegantly and tastefully decorated.

"When Sir Robert comes to stay, we have a staff of four regulars from the village. They have been coming for years and are accustomed to being called at a moment's notice. Sir Robert pays them a yearly retainer to keep them available, and they also come up occasionally to clean and air things out. Cora and I are just caretakers now and oversee the other staff, as we are getting up in years. I also putter around the grounds to keep the weeds away."

Holly could see that he loved the old place and was proud to show it. His wife showed them the library, the shelves of which held hundreds of volumes of leather bound books. Holly wondered aloud who dusted them all, and Cora McClure said she often came in with a feather duster, as the books had been her friends for years.

The massive oak table in the dining hall was at least thirty feet long. The table and chairs were covered with dust throws, but Holly's imagination could envision a huge banquet with the table groaning under mountains of food, the ladies in gorgeous silks and satin gowns, and the men in ruffles and bow ties. It was easy to dream in such a setting. Again there was a huge fireplace to lend the room atmosphere.

The music room was Holly's favourite. Tom said the grand piano dated back to the 1700s, and there was a beautiful old Irish harp that stood about six feet tall. Glass encased cupboards held violins and string instruments such as Holly had never seen before, and there was a beautifully carved white and gold harpsichord that dated back to Louis the Sixteenth. Tom pulled back the dust throws to let them look at this lovely furniture.

Tim was thrilled with the den, which boasted a bearskin rug. The walls were lined with trophies of the hunt, including a huge mounted tiger's head. Locked, glass encased cupboards displayed hundreds of weapons, both ancient and modern, each bearing a written detailed description of its origin. The trophies each bore the story of its capture.

There was a drawing room. Holly wasn't quite sure what it was used for, but there were a lot of little furniture groupings carefully placed to lend an air of intimacy. It was a friendly room.

An enormous kitchen was lined with many cupboards and, surprisingly, a large modern stove. Along one wall stood two deep freezers, each measuring about twelve feet long, and a huge refrigerator. Holly remarked that they looked out of place in such surroundings.

"Lord Mead had the freezers and refrigerator installed about thirty years ago. The stove is quite new," explained Mrs. McClure.

The bedrooms were furnished in beautiful antique furniture. Each room had a fireplace, and the walls were all wood panelling. Tom McClure explained that he had never shown anyone other than invited guests through before, and hoped that they would not talk about it in the village. Tim and Holly both promised him they wouldn't tell a soul and followed Mrs. McClure up the staircase to the second floor. There were hallways leading in several directions, and they followed her along the one that covered the west wing. Halfway down the corridor she stopped and took a key out of her pocket. She opened the door and stepped into the room, beckoning to them to follow her.

"This was my Lady Carolyn's room," she said softly. If I close my eyes, I can still see her in this room. She has never been far from my thoughts in all these years."

"Oh, what a gorgeous room!" exclaimed Holly.

There was no dust to be seen, and the room seemed lived in. Holly noticed the tears welling up in Mrs. McClure's eyes, and understood the love she had borne Lady Carolyn, the same love that had kept this room alive all these years.

How sad, she thought, *and how wonderful that such a love existed.*

Holly felt as though she was intruding on the others' thoughts. Tom McClure looked at his feet.

"Cora never gave up hope," he said. "Lady Carolyn was like her own child. She loved Cora more than she did Lady Mead, and Cora loved her. No one would ever have expected Lady Mead to take it so hard when Lady Carolyn disappeared. Her Ladyship was a very busy lady and had little time for the children."

As he spoke, Holly's gaze became riveted on an oil painting of a young girl. The painting hung over a green velvet settee, and Holly knew without asking that this was a portrait of Lady Carolyn. She had the strangest feeling that she had seen the girl before.

Suddenly, Holly understood the McClure's strange behaviour in offering to show her the castle. The girl in the painting was Holly's twin. Holly could have posed for it. Tim was just as astonished as Holly. He pointed at the painting and then at Holly, his mouth open in disbelief.

"When I saw you yesterday by the sundial," Mrs. McClure explained, "for a moment I thought my prayers had been answered, until I suddenly realized that forty years had passed since Lady Carolyn's disappearance. But the similarity was so startling that I knew I had to show you this painting. That's why I suggested the tour of the castle."

"Oh my goodness!" exclaimed Holly. "I wouldn't have believed this if I hadn't seen it with my own eyes." She stared at the painting as though mesmerized.

"I thought Cora had taken leave of her senses," said Tom, "when she told me about this yesterday, but as soon as I saw you this morning, I realized what she meant."

"Do you mind if I tell my grandmother and mom," asked Holly.

"No, of course you can tell them, but please don't tell anyone else," said Mrs. McClure. "Your grandmother probably thinks it strange that I offered to show you the castle."

"I thought it strange too," said Tim, "but now I understand. Don't worry, I won't tell anybody. I'm just glad that I was invited along."

Holly was wandering around, admiring the furniture. The room had an archway in the middle with heavy, green velvet drapes as a divider. One side was a sitting room and the other a bedroom. The bed was a large four poster and was covered with a green damask spread. There were three way mirrors on the dresser and a tapestry covered stool. A lovely old rocking chair stood in the corner, and the floors were covered with deep Persian rugs.

In contrast, the sitting room was very casual. A chaise recliner stood close to the fireplace, and several occasional chairs and small tables had been carefully placed to give the room a lived-in appearance. The settee was the only elegant piece of furniture in the room, but it lent itself to the décor very nicely.

Holly suddenly realized that everyone was waiting patiently for her to come out of her reverie. She apologized for lingering and followed the others into the corridor.

Tom McClure next showed them Lord and Lady Mead's suites. They were adjoining suites, but each had separate living and dining facilities. Holly thought it strange but decided not to ask questions. Dust throws were over everything, and it was apparent these rooms hadn't been lived in for many years. There were cobwebs around the windows and a great deal of dust.

They peeked into some of the other rooms in this wing and found them to be in the same condition. Then they backtracked and passed through several corridors until they found themselves in the old north wing. This part of the castle hadn't been used in over sixty years, and Holly experienced a creeping feeling as Tom brushed cobwebs aside to open one of the doors. The corridor was drafty and dark, and there was a cold dampness that made Holly shiver.

The door creaked on its hinges, and Holly was reminded of ghost and vampire movies as she half expected a bat to fly across the room. Rugs were rolled up and mildewed moulding throws were over everything. Nothing was in any apparent order, and the rotting smell of decay invaded the nostrils.

"These rooms are all like this," said Tom. "Some of them are empty and some are full of old trunks and rotting furniture."

"How many floors are there, Mr. McClure?" Holly asked.

"Four," said Tom, "but the top floor has never been used for anything but storage. There are rooms in the towers as well, but there's nothing in them."

They looked into several more rooms and found them to be in the same condition as the last one they saw. At one time, they must have been as elegant as the suite Sir Robert used.

Suddenly, just as they exited one of the rooms, a shadowy figure was seen to dart across the end of the corridor and vanish. Holly's heart jumped into her throat as Tom and Tim dashed off in pursuit.

"Who's there?" Tom yelled. "How did you get in here?"

Holly couldn't believe the old man could move so fast. Tim had trouble keeping up with him.

"Stay there, Holly and Cora. We'll catch this rascal," Tom yelled as he and Tim disappeared down the wide stone steps.

Holly's curiosity wouldn't allow her to wait, so she ran to the steps and watched as Tom and Tim disappeared around the curving stairway. It looked dark down there, and she hesitated about going any further.

"Better wait here, Holly," Mrs. McClure called. "Some of those steps are in need of repair, and there's no electricity in this part of the castle."

"Where do the steps lead to?" Holly inquired.

"There's a door on the main floor leading out to the courtyard, but it's kept locked. Another door leads into the old servants' quarters. The steps continue down from the main floor to the cellars, but this whole north wing hasn't been used in fifty or sixty years. I've no idea how anyone could get in here, as Tom has the only keys, except for Sir Robert, and he only carries one for the main door."

"How do the servants get in?" Holly asked.

"Tom lets them in and locks up when they leave," Cora said. "And as far as I know, there have been no keys given out to any of them, and none have been stolen."

"Cora! Are you there Cora?" Tom's voice reached out from the darkness below.

"Yes, Tom, Cora answered, "we're still here."

"We need lanterns. We'll be right up. We can't see a blessed thing down here." Tom was taking the steps two at a time as he spoke. Holly was amazed at his agility. Tim was behind him, and Holly could see the excitement in his eyes.

"We almost had him," said Tim, "but we lost him in the dark. He seemed to know his way around, though."

"Could you see who it was?" asked Mrs. McClure.

"No, he was in the shadows," said Tom, "and he moved like a cat. Let's go get some lanterns, and Tim and I will go back down and find him. For the life of me, I don't know how he got in. We'll lock the front door and come in through the courtyard and the old servants' quarters. Come on, Tim me boy, it'll be getting dark soon, and we don't want to be in here without some kind of light."

They made their way back along the corridor to the west wing and hurried down the stairs and through the great hall. Tom said they would have to continue the tour some other time. He locked the big double doors carefully and hurried around to the cottage with Tim in tow.

As Holly and Mrs. McClure arrived at the door of the cottage, he was already coming back out with two lanterns.

"Cora, you and Holly had better stay at the cottage. This fellow might be dangerous, and we don't want to give him a chance to cause any bloodshed. Keep the door locked, and stay out of sight. Just a minute, Tim." He signaled him to wait. "I'll be right back."

He disappeared into the house and came back out with a couple of clubs.

"We might need these," he warned Tim. "Better safe than sorry!"

Tom handed Tim a club, filled the lanterns with kerosene, and lit them. He adjusted the flame and handed one to Tim.

"Let's go now, Tim me lad, and be careful," he reminded him. "Don't take any chances. If you see him, clobber him, and don't wait to ask questions. The scoundrel is trespassing and could be armed with a weapon.

"Cora," he called over his shoulder, "better give Constable Millar a ring. Tell him we have a burglar and may need some help."

Tim was raring to go and had to be restrained by Tom, who cautioned him to take it easy. They went around the back of the castle, and Holly and Mrs. McClure went inside the cottage to wait.

Mrs. McClure phoned Constable Millar and relayed the message. The constable said he would come right away and would bring some help. There was never much excitement in Donnymead, and Constable Millar welcomed a chance to show his prowess as an enforcer of the law.

Pat Gallagher was clipping his hedge as Constable Millar came running out of the house and was immediately enlisted as Constable

Millar's assistant, mainly because he owned a taxi and the Constable had only a bicycle, and the road up to the castle was all uphill.

After a brief explanation, they were breaking the speed limits of Donnymead at the urging of the excited constable. In twelve minutes they pulled up in front of the castle and ran to the carriage house. Mrs. Brannigan and her daughter-in-law ran out when they saw the car. Upon realizing that something was wrong, they followed Pat and Constable Millar across the bridge.

"Pat! Constable Millar!" Mrs. Brannigan called after them. "What's wrong? Has something happened to Holly?"

When she saw Holly and Cora McClure at the door, she stopped running and gave a little cry of relief. Holly explained to them what had happened, while Cora McClure handed the men lanterns and a couple of heavy clubs and pointed the direction Tom and Tim had taken. Pat said he knew the way, and they hurried to find the men.

The ladies went into the cottage, and Cora put on the kettle to make some tea. Mrs. Brannigan introduced her daughter-in- law, Susan, to Mrs. McClure, and they settled down to wait for the men. Over a cup of tea and more of Mrs. McClure's delicious cakes, they discussed the events leading up to the discovery of the intruder. The ladies were particularly interested in Holly's account of the uncanny resemblance between Lady Carolyn and herself.

"All those years that I worked in the castle," mused Mrs. Brannigan, "and I've never been in Lady Carolyn's room. It was always kept locked, and of course Lady Carolyn had gone before I came. Such a tragedy for my poor Lady Mead to bear. She blamed herself for not paying enough attention to Lady Carolyn and believed that was the reason for her disappearance."

Holly was becoming bored with the chit chat and was relieved when she heard the men outside. She ran to the door, the others following behind, and discovered that the search had been in vain. The man had either managed to escape, or was still in the dungeons.

"I locked all of the doors leading into the castle from the cellars," said Tom. "If he's still down there, at least he won't be able to get into the castle and do any damage."

"We'll come back in the morning," said Pat, "and take another look. If he's still there, he should be glad to come out after a night in the dark." Constable Millar agreed. Tim and Holly made arrangements to meet the following morning when Tim delivered the milk. The cave was next on the agenda, and Holly wondered if tomorrow would be as exciting as today had been. Poor Tim had to drive the horse and cart back to the village by himself.

It was dark now, but the stars were out, and Tim assured Holly that if the prowler had managed to escape, he would not be foolish enough to hang around where so many were looking for him. Just to be on the safe side, Pat and Constable Millar promised to follow him in a few minutes after another quick look around the grounds.

Grandma Brannigan decided to lock all the windows and shutters, and she double locked the doors. The only one who seemed to be nervous was Holly's mother. Everyone else seemed to be enjoying the excitement.

That night, Holly wrote a letter to her best friend, Bonnie, in Vancouver. It was the first time she had ever written a nine page letter. Bonnie would think she had made it all up. Next, she dashed off a hurried letter to her father. It was a condensed version of the nine page letter to Bonnie and was crammed onto one page. She didn't read it over as she was afraid it might not make any sense, and she didn't feel like elucidating any further tonight.

What an incredible day it had been! Holly thought about all the things that had happened since she and Tim had left her grandmother's that morning. It was unbelievable that they had packed so much into one day. She really couldn't blame Bonnie if she didn't believe her letter.

The Cave

CHAPTER 5

TIM ARRIVED FOR HOLLY AT 8:30 THE FOLLOWING MORNING. SHE WAS JUST finishing her breakfast and was looking forward to exploring the cave. Tim told her to take her time, as he had to see if the McClure's wanted any dairy products. He also wanted to find out if there had been any new developments since the previous night with regard to the prowler incident.

When Tim returned, Holly was ready to go. He told them that Tom had not seen anything more of the prowler and intended to wait until Constable Millar and Tim's father arrived before investigating further.

"Pop has some deliveries to make this morning," said Tim, "but he promised to be out here by eleven o'clock. Constable Millar said he would rather wait until Pop was free. He said something about there being safety in numbers."

Holly's grandmother laughed heartily and said that she would be more useful in the search party than Constable Millar, and heaven help them if they were depending on the village protector for any kind of protection. When they pulled away from the gate, she was still chuckling gleefully, and Holly had a hilarious mental picture of Constable Millar hiding behind her grandmother's skirts.

The entrance to the cave was clearly visible this morning, and Tim said he hoped to be finished his rounds early. Holly sent her letters airmail and hoped they would arrive before her father left for Ireland. Tim stopped at Mr. Duffy's store to pick up some more milk and ice for the cooler. As Holly and Tim climbed down from the cart, Mr. Duffy came out of the store, followed by a radiant Casey.

He didn't look like the same boy Holly and Tim had left with Mr. Duffy only the day before. His clothes were new, and he had a fresh-scrubbed appearance. Obviously, Mrs. Duffy had a motherly hand in the transformation, and Holly and Tim could see that the boy was happy. He helped Mr. Duffy and Tim load up the cart, and as they were leaving he said, "Thank you, Mr. Tim and Miss Holly, for what you did for me. Mr. and Mrs. Duffy treat me awful good."

"I can see that, Casey," said Holly. "I'm so glad things are going better for you, and I hope Mr. Duffy will be able to find your Aunt Bessie for you."

"Me too," said Casey. "But Mr. Duffy says that if Aunt Bessie says it's alright, I can stay with him and Mrs. Duffy. He said I can go to school here and help him in the store Saturdays and holidays."

"Would you like that, Casey?" asked Holly.

"Oh yes, Miss Holly!" said Casey. "Aunt Bessie is a widow, and I would be just another mouth to feed. She's got three young 'uns like me, and I haven't seen her for four or five years. She's the only kin I have, but I think she'll be glad Mr. Duffy wants me."

"You bet I want him," said Mr. Duffy, who had been eavesdropping on the conversation. "Casey will be a big help to me. Mrs. Duffy and I get kind of lonely now that the family have grown and left us, and all we have to do to keep Casey happy is give him a chicken every Sunday."

Everybody, including Casey, laughed heartily. Holly and Tim wished him and Mr. Duffy good luck and hurried off to finish the milk deliveries.

"What a kind man," said Holly.

"Yes," agreed Tim. "Casey couldn't be in better hands."

Tim told Holly he had a delivery to make that morning to someone new in town.

"A Mr. Fryer has moved into the old Bailey place," he said. "Nobody seems to know anything about him, but Mr. Duffy said he seems to have plenty of money. He apparently drives a very expensive car, and he's been spending money like water."

They pulled up in front of a large, brown-stone house on the edge of the village. Tim went to the door and rang the bell. A thin man of medium height with blond, untidy hair answered the door.

"What do you want?" he said in a surly voice.

"Are you Mr. Fryer, Sir?" Tim inquired.

"What's it to you?" he snarled at Tim.

"I have a delivery for you, Sir, from Mr. Duffy's Store. Do you want it here or at the back door?"

"Bring it here; I'll take it," he said.

Tim went back to the cart and fetched the box of groceries.

"That'll be four pounds, ninety nine pence," said Tim as he handed Mr. Fryer the groceries.

"Hold on a minute then," said Fryer.

"Hey Dugan!" he shouted to someone inside. "Gi'me four pound, ninety nine for the groceries, and turn that blasted telly off. You can hear it in the next county."

"So what?" A big man had appeared in the doorway. "The telly is the only entertainment we have in this little burgh. If you watched it, Fryer, instead of pacing the floor, you wouldn't have such a filthy temper, and we wouldn't have to listen to you."

"Four, ninety nine you said?" he asked Tim. "Here you are, me lad, and here's fifty pence for you for delivering the groceries."

"Thank you very much, Sir," said Tim. "Have a fine day."

"That Mr. Fryer is a nasty bit of goods," said Tim to Holly as he climbed up onto the cart. "I wonder what they're doing in a little village like Donnymead?" he mused.

Tim finished the milk deliveries by 10:30 a.m. then they headed in the direction of the pier where Tim's father kept his boat moored. They decided to walk, as the pier was just a short distance from the village. There were several boats out just along the shore.

"What a glorious day," said Holly, as they walked down Ballymead Road. The sun was shining on the water, and several people waved to them as they passed by.

Holly liked the way Tim joked with some of the old people. Word had gotten around the village about her arrival from Canada, and she was the object of some curiosity. She was becoming accustomed to people greeting her as though they had known her all their lives.

"You've made quite a hit with the villagers, Holly," Tim remarked.

"Are they always so friendly?" Holly asked.

"Only when a beautiful colleen comes to the village," laughed Tim.

"Is that what you call 'blarney'?" Holly asked him.

"No," said Tim. "It was meant as a compliment."

"Well then," Holly curtseyed low, "thank you very much, kind Sir," and they both laughed merrily as she almost toppled over.

"I'm afraid I haven't had much practice in the art of curtseying," she grinned.

It was easy to spot Pat Gallagher's boat, as the name *Gallagher's Pride* was painted in bold letters on the side. Tim helped Holly climb aboard then untied the rope. As Holly settled down in the back of the boat, Tim fitted the oars in the locks and pulled away from the pier.

He rowed easily without effort, it seemed, and at his insistence Holly put on a life jacket. She told him she was a strong swimmer, but he insisted she wear it anyway. Tim rested his oars for a minute while he too slipped into a life jacket.

He explained that the currents could be treacherous, and if the boat capsized, they would be glad they were wearing jackets. At the moment, the waves looked very gentle, but he explained that this could change at a moment's notice.

"Better to be prepared, just in case a sudden storm happens to come up," Tim said.

The point was much farther away from the pier than it had appeared. Once they were around it, the rowing became much easier for Tim, and they made better progress. The cave entrance was much larger than it had looked from the road above, and Holly could feel the excitement building up in her. There were caves in the Rocky Mountains of British Columbia, but she had never been in one.

Holly was glad that Tim had brought the lanterns, as the cave looked dark and foreboding. Tim explained to her that the lanterns were better than flashlights, as batteries were apt to get damp, and then they wouldn't work. Besides, lanterns give a much better light.

Tim rowed right into the cave. The rocks rose gradually on either side of them, and Tim tied the boat to a sharp, jutting piece of rock by slipping a loop over the top and throwing in his anchor for added insurance. He helped Holly out of the boat, and they climbed up until they were on level ground.

Tim lit the lanterns, and the cave burst into a wonderland of colour and shadows. Massive rock formations rose up from the floor of the cave. Stalactites hung from the roof like giant icicles, and helictites branched out in every direction like an enchanted forest beckoning irresistibly to them, daring them to explore her hidden secrets. As Holly and Tim held the lanterns aloft, the reflection of the light playing on the colours reminded Holly of a huge cathedral.

"Holy Toledo, Tim!" she exclaimed in an awestruck voice not much above a whisper. "Have you ever in your life seen anything like this?"

"Well, I've been here several times with Pop when I was younger, but Pop isn't an explorer by nature, and we never spent too much time looking around. I never came out by myself, because exploring isn't any fun if you're by yourself. We're so used to having the cave that we don't really appreciate it the way tourists and visitors do. Most people are afraid of being trapped in here by the tide, so they don't stray too far from the entrance. There are many caves along the coasts of Ireland," he went on, "and around The Giant's Causeway, there are magnificent underground caverns."

Holly started walking toward the back of the cave, holding her lantern high in front of her. Tim followed her and warned her to be careful of her footing as she stepped onto a ledge that wound around a giant column. They followed the ledge around until they came to another ledge. Holly climbed up and then screamed in terror as something flew past her head with a wild flapping of wings.

"It's alright, Holly," Tim assured her as he reached out for her hand. "It's just a bat. The light scared it," he explained. "They like the dark, so it'll be in a dark corner by now. There are hundreds of them in here. That's another reason people aren't too interested in exploring the cave. Most people are scared to death of bats."

"Well, I'm not going to let them stop me," said Holly. "I may never get another chance like this." She crouched down, half expecting another bat to swoop down on her, but nothing happened.

"This is fantastic, Tim." She stood up, a little more brave now. "Look at this big mushroom shaped stalagmite. I learned about these in school. The colours come from the different minerals that coat the limestone. Wow!" she exclaimed excitedly. "Look at that orange and purple rock there. Isn't it super?"

Holly was ecstatic and climbed from one rock to another, waving her lantern back and forth, revelling in the explosion of colour. Tim enjoyed watching her, and he followed as she climbed from ledge to ledge. Suddenly, he realized that they had been climbing up and the floor of the cave was far beneath them.

"Holly," he cautioned her, "we'd better not go any further. It will be harder to climb back down in the dark."

"Wait a minute, Tim!" Holly gasped. "There's some kind of passage here. Can we take a look?"

"Hey, you're right. Wow," exclaimed Tim. "I've never been up here before. Let's see how far the passage goes," he suggested.

"Isn't this exciting?" Holly was already walking cautiously along the passage. The walls were steep and smooth, and Holly could taste the dank odour in her throat. The air seemed to be thin and stale as well.

"Take it easy, Holly!" Tim warned. "There might be crevices in the floor of the passage."

"Don't worry," she replied. "You're right! I wouldn't want to disappear. I'll be more careful. Hey, here's another passage off to my right."

"Let's just follow this one, Holly, and be careful. You never know what's up ahead."

"Right, Tim," she agreed. "How about this?" She picked up a paper bag that was lying in her path and checked inside. It was empty.

"It looks as though we aren't the only ones who know about this passage. Somebody else has been along here and quite recently. This bag isn't damp or musty. Do you think it might be someone from the village?"

"I don't think so," said Tim. "I've never heard anyone talk about it, and you know what villagers are like—they can't keep anything a secret for very long."

"What's this, Tim? Hey," Holly exclaimed, "there's a big room to my left. Look at that Tim," Holly cried eagerly. "There are a lot of boxes in there."

Tim held his lantern up beside Holly's to look at the huge chamber. It was weird and eerie, and smelled damp and musty.

"Somebody's been here alright," whispered Holly. "I wonder what's in those boxes," she said fearfully.

"Let's take a look," Tim suggested.

He shone the lantern on the boxes. There were letters on the side of them.

"Dynamite!" they both exclaimed simultaneously. They looked at each other, and Holly could feel herself start to shiver and shake.

"Those boxes look new," said Tim. "They can't have been here very long, and here's a box full of guns. Wow!"

The horrendous implications of such a find struck both Holly and Tim at the same time.

"I'd better tell my Pop about this. Come on, Holly. Let's go!" Tim urged.

They hurried down the passageway and started their climb down to the floor of the cave. Suddenly, Tim stopped and shone his lantern around the cave.

"Holly!" Tim's voice was very strange. Holly was quick to catch the note of alarm. "Don't get scared, but the entrance is almost covered with water. There isn't room for the boat to pass through. We'll have to stay up here until the tide goes out."

"Oh, it's all my fault, Tim," she wailed. "If I hadn't insisted on climbing higher and then checking out the passage, this would never have happened. How long do you think we'll be in here?"

"Probably for several hours," said Tim. "Well, we might as well go back up and explore the rest of the passages. We have lots of oil in the lanterns, and I'm interested in anything else that we might find up there."

"I guess you're right, Tim," agreed Holly. "There's no sense in wasting the time that we're stuck here."

She started climbing again when suddenly she thought about the boat.

"What will happen to the boat, Tim?"

"Oh, the boat will be alright. It'll just rise with the water."

"Thank goodness," Holly said. "I was afraid we might have to swim for it, and from what you tell me about the currents, it doesn't sound too safe."

They reached the top and found the passage without difficulty. This time they continued on past the chamber that concealed their ominous find. Tim had taken Holly's hand, as he realized she was a little frightened now considering the circumstances. Suddenly, they discovered there were steps ahead of them—a lot of steps.

"I wonder where they lead to," said Tim. "Well, there's only one way to find out. Are you game, Holly?"

Holly shivered.

"Of course I am," she said bravely. "Oh wow, Bonnie will never believe this."

"Who's Bonnie?" asked Tim.

"My best friend," she whispered.

For some reason she had the feeling she'd better whisper. Who knew what might be up ahead? Holly had been in sticky situations before, but this was incredible.

There were at least a hundred steps. They were definitely man-made. Huge stones and rocks had been used in their construction, and they were probably several centuries old. They led up to a trap door, which moved easily when Tim pushed up against it.

He moved it aside and set his lantern inside the hole. Pulling himself up, he took a quick look around.

"What's up there, Tim?" Holly asked anxiously.

"I'm not sure, but I think we're in the dungeons below the castle. Give me your lantern and I'll help you up."

"What if the prowler is still up there?" Holly said in a frightened whisper.

"We'll have to take that chance, Holly," said Tim. "Come on! We've come this far, let's not panic now."

She reached the lantern up to him and scrambled through the hold. The trap door had a steel ring on it, and Tim fitted it back over the hole.

"I wouldn't want either of us to fall down the hole and break our necks," he explained. "Now let's see if we can get out of here. Let's follow this passage and see where it leads us."

He took Holly's hand again and she followed him like a little lamb. The dark shadows were really frightening. Her imagination was running wild, and her heart was stuck in her throat. She was expecting at any moment a wild figure to jump out of the shadows, wielding a knife or a gun. At the moment, she never wanted to see the cave again.

They reached the end of the passage, which was blocked by a heavy wooden door.

"I hope it isn't locked," said Tim as he tried the latch. It wouldn't budge. It was locked. Tim started banging on it and kicking.

"Come on, Holly! Kick the door! There's just a chance that Tom McClure might be in the castle, though I doubt that he would hear us down here."

Holly was happy to join him, and between the two of them, they made quite a noise. They kept it up for several minutes then suddenly they heard the door being opened. Holly gave a little squeal and jumped backward.

"Who's in there?" shouted Tom McClure.

"It's me, Mr. McClure—Tim Gallagher."

"The devil you say," exclaimed Tom as he opened the door. "Tim, me lad, and Miss Holly, how the devil did you get in there?"

Pat Gallagher and Constable Millar were behind Tom, clubs raised and ready to do battle.

"It's a long story, Mr. McClure," said Tim. "Boy, am I glad to see you, Pop. You wouldn't believe what we found."

Tim proceeded to tell the men how they happened to be there, and how he and Holly had discovered the dynamite and guns. Constable Millar looked a bit sick. Tim offered to show them where the cache was hidden.

Tim and Holly led the way through the trapdoor and down the steps. The men were flabbergasted and excited. This was quite a discovery for them to make.

"Can you beat that," said Pat as they gazed dumbfounded at the huge chamber. "I've lived in Donnymead all my life and I never knew these passages and chambers were here."

"Neither did I," said Tom. "The dungeons have never been used in all the years I've worked here, so I had no reason to be in them. I locked that door last night when we were down here. Good thing for you two that we were looking for that blackguard who was here yesterday. Well, it's obvious how he got in and out, and he must have had something to do with this arsenal here."

The others agreed with him, and they also agreed they would have to make plans in order to catch the culprits. It was obvious that there had to be more than one man involved, as it would be impossible for one man to transport all the boxes of heavy equipment from a boat to the cave and then up to its present location. Those involved were certainly up to no good. That was the unanimous consensus of the group.

The men counted the boxes and found there to be fifteen boxes of dynamite and twelve boxes of rifles. There was no ammunition, but there were four boxes of caps and fuses.

"I don't know what we're going to do about this, but whatever we decide, we'd better do it quickly," said Tom. "Let's go folks," he urged. "Let's get back to daylight where we can think. My mind seems to be boggled down here."

Tom led the way this time back up to the dungeons. He was very careful to lock all the doors behind them. The cells had bars on the doors, and the place gave Holly the creeps as cobwebs brushed her face.

They seemed to walk forever down dark passages and through a huge wine cellar until they came to the stairway leading up to the servants' quarters. Holly and Tim raced on ahead.

"Oh, I'm so glad to see daylight," Holly cried with relief.

"Me too," said Tim. "Jeepers, what a day!" he exclaimed.

They sat down on the top step, cupped their heads in their hands, and waited for the others.

The Treasure Box

CHAPTER 6

MRS. MCCLURE HAD MADE TEA FOR THE GROUP, AND SHE LISTENED AND ASKED questions as they discussed the day's events. There was a great deal of controversy as to the reason for the dynamite and guns being concealed in the cavern. The more they discussed it, the more outlandish the conclusions were. One thing they all agreed on, however, was that something criminal was afoot.

They decided to call a meeting of those men of the village who could be trusted—the village council. The dynamite and guns would have to be moved to a safe place until authorities in Belfast were notified and could decide what to do with them. Constable Millar had psyched himself right out. He spilled his tea twice, and Mrs. McClure had to keep pouring for him and wiping up the spills.

Holly had gotten over her scare and enjoyed being a part of the excitement. Suddenly, she remembered something that had been in the back of her mind, but in all the excitement she had forgotten to mention to Mrs. McClure.

"Mrs. McClure," she cried, "I almost forgot. Don't you think it strange that the gypsy told me about all of these incidents before they happened? How could she know about the tunnels or passages? And something else I forgot about that I think we should check out is that loose stone that she said we would find in the fireplace with the box behind it. Do you think we might check Lady Carolyn's room?"

Cora McClure was already looking for the keys.

"I completely forgot about that, Holly," she exclaimed, "what with everything that's been happening around here. Come on, Tom," she pleaded, "I won't rest till I see if there's anything to this. Too many of the other predictions have come true to ignore this one."

"There's something strange about those gypsies, I have to admit that," said Tom. "Alright, Cora," he said resignedly, "I can see there's no use arguing with you. Let's go take a look. You might as well all come along," he nodded to the others. "I don't know what Sir Robert would say if he knew what was going on. I'm just glad he's not here."

They all followed Tom back into the castle, this time through the front doors. Pat Gallagher and Constable Millar walked as though they were on hallowed ground. Pat had been in the castle before, but never through the front door. They had always called him when something went wrong with the plumbing or the generator, but he had always used the servants' entrance.

Tom led the way up the lovely marble staircase, along the balcony, and down the corridor to Lady Carolyn's room. Once in the room, Holly could see the surprise on Pat Gallagher's and Constable Millar's faces when they saw how beautifully it had been kept, but they refrained from comment.

Tom moved immediately to the fireplace and started to feel for the loose stone. He prodded and pushed every stone and had almost finished examining them all when, suddenly, a stone at the bottom right hand corner moved slightly at this touch. He looked at his wife and then took a pocket knife out of his pocket. It took a little prying and tugging, but the stone came away with very little effort. Holly and Tim were already on their knees, and Holly could see that there was something in the hole.

"I see it, Mr. McClure!" she gasped with delight. "There's a box in there."

"You're right, Miss Holly," said Tom, and he pulled it out and carried it over to one of the little tables.

"Why, I remember that box," cried Cora. "Lady Carolyn used to call it her treasure box."

The box was an ornate design, much like the old fashioned music boxes, and was about twelve inches long by six inches wide and four or five inches deep. Tom opened it easily, as it wasn't locked. There was some costume jewelry in it and a book.

Cora picked up the book and fingered it lovingly. "This was her diary," she said softly. "I wonder if there's anything in it that might give us a clue to her disappearance."

"I don't think we should read it, Cora," warned Tom.

"I will take responsibility for reading the diary," said Cora firmly. "Lock the jewelry up, Tom. I'll put the book back when I'm finished with it."

Tom could see that Cora had made up her mind and the subject was closed. He put the stone back in place and picked up the box. When they were all back in the corridor, he locked the door again. A sort of stunned silence had fallen over the group. Holly nudged Tim.

"Tim," she whispered. "I'd like to see the gypsy lady again. Do you think maybe we could go tomorrow?"

"I was thinking the same thing, Holly. All these predictions must be more than just coincidence." He looked at his watch. "It's supper time now, but I'll be back in the morning, and we'll go to the gypsy camp right after I've finished my milk deliveries. Pop and I will have to go and get the boat when the tide is out. We can take Mr. Duffy's boat. He's got one with a motor, so we won't take so long in getting back to the cave."

"Well, so long, Tim. Mom and Grandma will be wondering what's happened to me. I suppose if I tell them of our adventure they'll worry more about me."

Tom locked up the jewelry in the library. The others were preparing to leave, so Holly said goodbye and headed for her grandmother's. What a day it had been! Yesterday, too! It was incredible.

Her dad would have loved every minute of it. He loved intrigue or a good mystery. *Too bad he wasn't here*, she thought. Her mom was different. She didn't have any sense of adventure in her. She always liked things to be safe, and she worried about Holly's unending quest for excitement.

Her grandmother saw her coming and met her at the door.

"Holly dear," she was puzzled. "How on earth did you get in there without me seeing you?"

"It's a long story, Grandma, and you'll never believe it," said Holly.

"Well, your supper is ready, child. Call your mother, and you can tell us all about it. She's in her room freshening up."

Holly was about to knock on her mother's door when the door opened.

"Oh, Holly!" she exclaimed. "I thought I heard your voice. My goodness, dear, we hardly ever see you these days." Her mother was putting on a necklace as she spoke. "Help me with this, dear. I can't seem to find the clasp."

Holly fastened the necklace and apologized to her mother for being late. She hurried to wash up, as she was bursting with the news of her day's adventures. As usual, her grandmother had outdone herself, and the meal was a masterpiece. But when Holly gave her account of the day's escapades, her mother and grandmother suddenly lost their appetites. Her mother kept saying, "Oh, I wish your father were here."

"What on earth are they going to do about the dynamite and guns?" her grandma asked.

"I don't know, Grandma," said Holly. "I heard them say they were going to call a meeting of the village council and decide what to do about it. If Dad were here, he would know what to do."

"Aye, child," Grandma agreed. "I'd feel a lot safer if David were here. Tom's a good fellow, but it's not the same as having a man in the house when there's trouble. Dynamite and guns!" she exclaimed. "What's the world coming to?"

Holly told them about the box they found and how Mrs. McClure was going to read the diary.

"Well, I suppose if anybody has a right to read it, Cora has," said her grandma. "Though I can't see why she'd want to keep bringing back the past."

They were just finishing supper when the telephone rang. Grandma Brannigan answered it.

"Who did you say it was? The overseas operator? Yes, this is Mrs. Mary Brannigan ... David? Oh, David, it's so good to hear your voice.

Hold on a minute, David ... It's David on the phone," she called over her shoulder, "phoning from Vancouver. Yes, David! They're here now. Oh, you wouldn't believe the things that have been going on. I wish you were here, David ... Susan? Yes, I'll put her on. Susan! David wants to speak to you." She handed the phone to Holly's mother.

"Hello, David. Oh, I'm so relieved to hear your voice."

"How are you, dear?" David's voice was very faint.

"I can barely hear you, David," Susan said. "We're fine, but we miss you terribly. Some dreadful things have been happening to Holly. She got trapped in the cave by the tide, and then she was stuck in some underground passages with dynamite and guns and had to be rescued. Oh, I wish you were here, David," she wailed.

"Mom," cried Holly, "give me the phone. You'll scare Dad to death. Hello, Dad!"

"Holly?" her Dad sounded alarmed. "What's all this about dynamite and guns and being trapped in the cave?"

"I'm all right, Daddy. There's a great mystery here right now. It has to do with the castle. We're going to see the gypsy again tomorrow, and maybe they'll catch the prowler soon, and the mystery will be solved."

"My goodness, Holly," Mr. Brannigan was shouting now, "has everyone there gone mad? Never mind. I'll be on the plane tomorrow, and I'll get to the bottom of this. Let me talk to your mother again. And Holly, try to keep out of trouble till I get there!"

Holly handed the phone to her mother. She wondered why her dad had become so alarmed. Still, she was glad he was coming tomorrow instead of next Monday as he had planned. Her mother was crying with relief when she hung up the phone.

"Oh, thank goodness David is coming tomorrow," she exclaimed as she dabbed her eyes with a handkerchief.

Holly couldn't quite see what all the fuss was about. She knew her father well enough to know that he would soon be caught up in the excitement. Her father was in an exciting business and enjoyed a certain amount of danger; however, if she or her mother were involved in anything dangerous ... well, he could be a little alarmed. But since she was planning to be a criminal lawyer someday, any experience she could glean in that particular area would be to her advantage. Her mother would like her to choose a less dangerous career, but her father was proud of her choice and hoped that some day they would be partners.

It was going to be difficult for Holly to wait until tomorrow for him to arrive. What on earth would she do with her time this evening? She decided to go out to the Point and enjoy the scenery for awhile. Her mother and grandma would be happy to know she was going to be around this evening.

Holly and her mother did the dishes while her grandma tidied up and put the dishes away.

"What are you planning to do this evening, Holly?" her mother asked with a note of apprehension in her voice.

"Don't worry, Mom." Holly tried to calm her mother's fears. "I'm just going to the Point to watch the boats. You'll be able to see me from the house."

"Thank heaven for that." Her mother was relieved. "Try and stay out of trouble until your father arrives."

"Why does everyone keep saying that to me?" Holly exclaimed in exasperation.

Her grandmother laughed heartily, and her mother even managed a flicker of a smile. Holly put on her windbreaker and kissed her mother and grandmother goodbye.

"I won't be long, Mom," she said as she went out the door.

The weather was heavenly, and Holly strolled leisurely in the direction of the Point, stopping occasionally to pick primroses, bluebells, and buttercups. There were so many beautiful wild flowers, and the grass was so green everywhere she looked. It was no wonder people sang songs about the forty shades of green.

When she reached the Point, Holly sat down on a rock and turned her attention to the cave. She was just in time to see Tim and his father as they emerged from the entrance. They were in a larger boat, which was powered by a motor, and they had the little rowboat in tow. Holly waved to them, but they didn't see her, and she watched as they rounded the Point and headed in to the pier.

The sea was calm. The little wavelets barely made a splash as they played around the rocks below. Holly could see several fishing boats trolling just behind the rocks. She had gone fishing with her dad many times around the Vancouver coast. Lion's Bay and Horseshoe Bay had been great for ling cod. They were horrible looking fish, but great to eat. She wondered what kind of fish they were catching down below. Her dad would be thrilled to be out there.

Suddenly, a motor boat seemed to appear out of nowhere. It rounded the point at great speed and headed straight for the cave. Just before reaching the entrance to the cave, it slowed down. Holly counted three men. She couldn't be sure from this height, but she thought two of them looked familiar.

The Point hid them from the view of the other boats, but Holly could see them very well. Something about their furtive behavior caused Holly to lie flat on her stomach, and she cautiously peeked over the edge of the cliff.

The boat seemed to be loaded with boxes. Holly's heart almost stopped beating as she remembered the boxes in the chamber of the cave. She watched as the boat disappeared into the cave. Holly jumped to her feet and started running toward the castle. She must tell Tom McClure about this. Maybe they were the men he was looking for. She was barely touching the ground as she ran through the gate past her grandmother's cottage and headed for the bridge. Tom was raking some leaves in the garden when she burst through the bridge shed.

"What on earth is after you, Holly?" Tom was leaning his rake against a tree as he spoke.

"Mr. McClure, come quick! I just saw three men in a motor boat going into the cave." Holly was almost gasping for breath.

"Lots of people go into the cave, Holly," said Tom.

"But they had a lot of boxes piled up in the boat, Mr. McClure, and they were acting very suspicious," Holly explained.

At her reference to the boxes, Tom McClure suddenly became interested.

"Where were you when you saw this?" he inquired.

"Down at the Point," she said eagerly.

"Let's go take a look," Tom said.

He was already on his way, taking long strides like a panther. Holly was running and had trouble keeping up with him. When they reached the point, there was no one in sight around the cave, so they settled down to wait.

"You say there were three of them, Holly?" he questioned.

Holly nodded in affirmation. She was afraid to speak, as she knew from having spent so much time on the water with her father that sound carries across water, though she didn't know if that would apply from this height.

"There wouldn't be much I could do against three men who are probably armed if they are connected with that arsenal in the cave, but maybe we can find out who they are, and we can let the authorities handle it. By the time we could get someone out from the village, they would probably be gone. We'll have to organize something at the meeting tomorrow night, so we can set up shifts to stake the cave out. We'll have to be ready in case there's a fight."

They waited about an hour. Suddenly, they saw the boat leave the cave.

"The boxes are gone, Mr. McClure," Holly whispered excitedly.

"Are you sure they were there?" he asked.

"Yes, I'm positive!" she exclaimed. "They were piled up high in the boat."

"Well, there's nothing there now," Tom observed. "It's difficult to tell from this distance, but I don't believe I have ever seen those men before."

"I think I have," said Holly. "Tim made a grocery delivery to some new customers in town, and I think I recognize two of them. One was called Dugan, and the other was called Fraser, or Flyer. No! I remember now. It was Fryer. I remember Tim calling him by name. He had a lame foot. His right shoe was built up, and Tim said he was a very nasty man."

"Well, in that case," said Tom in a low voice, "we better not alert them until we have enough men for a confrontation. Apparently, they have unloaded some more weapons for storage in the cave. They appear to be very dangerous men, though I can't believe the weapons are meant for use against our little village. There isn't even a bank in Donnymead that they might rob, and none of the villagers are wealthy. We'd better get back home," he suggested, "and I'll call Pat Gallagher and Jim Duffy to arrange a meeting for tomorrow night. It'll take time to round everybody up."

"Dad will be here tomorrow," said Holly. "He's a criminal lawyer and is accustomed to investigating every kind of crime. I'm sure he would be glad to help."

"We'd appreciate any professional help we can get. We seldom have any criminal activity in Donnymead, so we don't have the police force to handle it at this time."

Tom said goodnight to Holly and hurried off to make his telephone calls. Holly went into the cottage. She had seen her grandma and mother at the window and knew they were dying with curiosity.

"What have you been up to now, Holly?" her mother inquired. "And why was Mr. McClure with you?"

Holly told them excitedly of the latest developments in the mystery. Her grandmother was enjoying it immensely, but her mother acted like she was on the verge of a nervous breakdown.

"We haven't had this much excitement in twenty years," said Grandma Brannigan. "I wonder what they're going to do with the guns and dynamite?" she mused.

"I don't know, Grandma," said Holly. "Mr. McClure can't figure out what those men might want to use it for. He's calling a meeting of the village council to decide what's to be done."

"Well, we have more than our share of what you call 'excitement' in Vancouver," said Susan, "and David always seems to be in the middle of it. Holly has scared me to death a few times," she went on. "She has a knack for sniffing out trouble, just like her father. For instance, last year when they smashed a dope ring in her school, she helped the police in the investigation."

"My! You really do have a nose for trouble, don't you child?" Her grandmother seemed proud of her. "But then, you wouldn't be David's daughter if you didn't have the soul of an adventurer in you."

Holly spent the rest of the evening preparing for the next day. Her grandma made a lunch for her and Tim after Holly told her she didn't expect to be back before the middle of the afternoon. She dug her camera out and put a film in it.

The gypsies would make terrific subjects if they would permit her to take pictures. The camera was an Olympus Trip 35 with an electronic flash. Her father had given it to her for Christmas, and it took marvellous pictures. She also wanted to get a picture of the beautiful horse that she had seen the gypsy, Anthony, riding.

The castle was another subject. She hoped to take a couple of films of the castle itself and the cave as well, depending on whether or not she would be able to make another trip to it before going home. It was much too dangerous at the present time, but if the men were caught and the mystery unravelled, she would definitely ask Tim to take her back, and they would explore all of the passages at their leisure.

At 9:45 the phone rang. Grandma Brannigan answered it. It was Cora McClure, and she wanted to talk to Holly.

"Hi, Mrs. McClure," Holly greeted her.

"Hello, Holly!" Mrs. McClure sounded excited. "Could I ask a favour of you, dear?"

"Of course, Mrs. McClure. What can I do for you?"

"I'd like to go into the village in the morning. Would you ask Tim when he comes if I could go with him?"

"Certainly, Mrs. McClure, I'm sure he won't mind," Holly assured her.

"Thank you, dear. Goodbye now."

Holly stared into space as she hung up the phone.

"Something wrong, dear?" her grandma asked.

"No." Holly's brow was puckered. "At least I don't think so. Mrs. McClure wants to ride in with us in the morning. She sounded so strange, though. Oh, it's probably just my imagination."

It had been a long, full day, so Holly decided to have her bath and go to bed early. Her grandmother had lit the fire in her bedroom to take the chill off the night air. As she lay in bed, the firelight danced and formed pictures in her mind's eye. In the flickering shadows, she could see a castle and a huge black horse prancing as though to music.

Sinister Undertones

CHAPTER 7

THE SUN WAS SHINING AND THE BIRDS WERE SINGING WHEN HOLLY AWOKE. SO much had happened that it was hard to believe it was only Thursday. Eight o'clock! Tim would be here soon! She jumped out of bed and dressed quickly.

Thank goodness she had set her clothes out the night before. Breakfast was ready when she came downstairs. Her mother was still in bed, and Holly tapped on her door to let her know breakfast was on the table.

"Good morning, Grandma," she announced. "It's a glorious morning, isn't it?"

"That it is, child. It rained a little during the night, just enough to freshen everything in the garden. What have you planned for today, dear?"

"We're going to see the gypsies again, and I'm going to take dozens of photographs. I want to take some pictures of you later on, Grandma."

"In that case, I'd better put on my best bib and tucker," her grandma laughed.

Holly had almost finished her breakfast when her mother came into the kitchen. She was in her dressing gown and still looked tired.

"You look as though you haven't slept all night," said Grandma Brannigan.

"You're right, Mother Brannigan. I hardly slept at all," she sighed. "I couldn't get all of these goings on out of my mind. I'll be glad to see David today."

"Well, eat your breakfast, dear, and maybe you'll feel better. Maybe you'll be able to sleep later on."

"What kind of shenanigans are you going to be up to today, Holly?" her mother asked.

Holly was laughing. "Shenanigans!" she exclaimed. "Mom, you're beginning to talk like the Irish," she teased.

Her grandmother fussed over her mother. It wasn't much fun for her mom with Dad so far away, especially since it was almost two miles into the village, and her grandma didn't own a car. There was a knock on the door, and Cora McClure came in.

"Good morning, folks. I hope I'm not too early," she said. She was dressed in a dark green suit and had obviously taken great pains with her hair. Everyone said hello, and Grandma Brannigan poured her a cup of tea.

"What an attractive suit that is," observed Susan.

"Thank you, my dear." Mrs. McClure looked pleased. "I bought it for my niece's wedding a couple of years ago and haven't worn it since. I decided I'd better start getting some wear out of it before the moths take a fancy to it."

A clatter outside indicated that Tim had arrived. He came in smiling as usual and greeted everyone cheerfully.

"Well, good morning, everybody, I see you're ready to go, Holly," he said.

"Right, Tim, Mrs. McClure would like a ride into the village. Okay?"

"Sure! Anytime you want to ride in with me, Mrs. McClure, you're very welcome," said Tim. "How are you going to get back?"

"I'll get Pat to bring me back in the taxi."

"Oh, I almost forgot," Grandma Brannigan exclaimed. "Will you ask Pat to meet the bus, Tim? Holly's daddy will be here this afternoon."

"Will do," said Tim. "That's the four o'clock bus, isn't it?"

"That's right," said Grandma.

She bought some milk and cream, and Mrs. McClure bought butter and eggs and milk.

"Do you mind if I leave these here, Mary? I can pick them up when I come home."

"Of course you can, Cora. Don't forget your lunch basket, Holly," she reminded her granddaughter.

"Thank you, Grandma." Holly took the basket and put her camera strap over her shoulder. She kissed her mother and grandma and headed for the door.

"Don't be late, dear," her mother warned. "Remember, your father is coming."

"Don't worry, Mom," she promised. "We'll be back in plenty of time."

Tim helped Mrs. McClure up beside him on the cart, and Holly sat on the outside. She told Tim of her previous evening's discovery. Mrs. McClure had already heard of it from Tom, but she was enjoying Holly's version of it.

"I heard Pop talking about it last night on the phone," said Tim. "There's going to be a meeting to decide what should be done."

"Just think, Holly," said Mrs. McClure, "if you hadn't come here on a holiday, we probably would never have known what was going on right under our noses. Who knows what these evil men have in mind."

"We'd better get a move on," said Tim, as he urged the horse to a trot. "I made most of my deliveries early this morning, so we can start out for the gypsy camp about ten o'clock. I have to make another delivery to that Mr. Fryer this morning, and a couple of others on the edge of town, and then I'll be finished."

Mrs. McClure looked startled.

"You say you are going to the gypsy camp again, Tim?" she asked anxiously.

"Yes," Tim replied. "Don't worry, Mrs. McClure," he went on. "They're very friendly ... not at all what I would expect gypsies to be like."

"That's right," Holly assured her. "The princess invited us back to see her. She is a lovely person. Her son, Anthony, is a strange one, though. He appears to be well educated, but he has a very arrogant manner."

Mrs. McClure laughed.

"An arrogant, educated gypsy? Now there's one for the books. By the way, Holly," she added, "I'm looking forward to seeing your father. I've known him since he was a baby. We're all very proud of his success in Canada."

"Thank you," Holly acknowledged the compliment. "Daddy has done well for himself. Someday I hope to become his partner, and the firm will be called Brannigan and Brannigan."

"Very impressive," said Mrs. McClure. "I do hope you achieve your ambition, Holly. That's a very high goal to set for yourself, but Mary tells me you are a straight 'A' student. I wish you luck, my dear."

"Thank you, Mrs. McClure."

"A straight 'A' student?" said Tim. "Wow, you must be a brain."

"Not really," Holly blushed. "I have to study hard for my grades, but I'm determined to make the bar someday, and you can't do that by goofing off."

"We're almost there," said Tim. "Where would you like to get off, Mrs. McClure?"

"Duffy's store will be fine," she replied.

When Tim pulled up in front of the store, Mrs. McClure thanked him, and Tim helped her down. As the horse ambled on down the street, Holly and Tim waved goodbye as Mrs. McClure disappeared inside the store. In half an hour, Tim was finished his milk deliveries and went back to the store to unload the ice and leftover milk.

Mr. Duffy had a bag of groceries ready for delivery to Mr. Fryer, and Mrs. McClure had already left the shop. Casey was singing off-key as he helped Tim unload the cart. Holly was happy for Casey and hoped that his aunt would give him permission to stay with Mr. and Mrs. Duffy. It was obviously a very happy arrangement for all concerned.

When they were on their way again, Holly and Tim discussed Mr. Fryer and friends and wondered aloud if they could possibly find out anything about them while delivering the groceries. By the time they pulled into Mr. Fryer's driveway, they still hadn't come up with a plan.

Tim decided to go to the back door this time, and Holly went along with him. Her curiosity wouldn't permit her to stay on the cart. As they rounded the back of the house, loud, angry voices assailed them. They stopped automatically and crouched down just below the kitchen window. Mr. Fryer's voice was very belligerent.

"If you two aren't more careful, you're going to blow this whole deal. The villagers aren't stupid, you know."

"You worry too much, Fryer." Tim recognized the voice of the man called Dugan. "They haven't caught on so far, and we've been haulin' the stuff right under their noses."

A twig snapped in the bushes behind Holly and Tim, and they almost stopped breathing, but nothing happened.

"Must've been a cat or dog," whispered Tim.

"Wow, I can hear my heart pounding," whispered Holly. "Maybe this isn't such a good idea."

"Shush!" Tim put his finger to his lips.

"I saw those two up on the cliffs when we came out of the cave last night," Fryer's voice went on. "We should have waited till after dark to move the stuff."

"Well," Dugan's voice again, "we move the rest of it tonight, and by midnight, we'll have it off our hands for good."

Holly was wondering where the third man was when, suddenly, she and Tim both froze. They sensed rather than heard someone behind them. A big hand clamped down on each of their shoulders, and Holly thought she was going to faint dead away. It was evident that the third man had found them.

"Well, well, well … what have we here?"

They looked up at a pair of blazing eyes. He was a big man. From where they crouched, he looked like a mountain.

"Fryer! Dugan!" he shouted. "We've got company! Come on you two—inside!"

He yanked Tim and Holly to their feet and pushed them ahead of him through the back door.

"I found them listening under the back window," he explained. "Anybody could hear you two a block away!"

"I told you, Fryer," Dugan said sharply, "that your loud mouthed temper would get us in trouble."

"Shut up, Dugan! Let me think. What were you two doing out there, anyway?" he demanded.

"We were delivering your groceries, Sir," answered Tim.

"Why were you crouched under the window if you were delivering groceries?" Fryer asked.

"It's my fault, Sir," Holly tried to explain. "I dropped some money, and Tim was helping me look for it."

"That's right, Sir," Tim agreed. "It rolled into the bushes."

It was a feeble attempt, and Tim and Holly knew it.

"Well, it's a cinch we can't let them go, at least not until after tonight's delivery."

Fryer was pacing the floor as he spoke.

"Take them down to the cellar and lock them up, Moore. We'll decide what to do with them after midnight tonight. We have too much to do to worry about two brats at this stage of the game. Give me the groceries, boy," he said to Tim, "and no tricks. If you behave yourselves, you just might get out of this alive," he warned them.

"Come on, Dugan!" said Moore. "Gi'me a hand with these two little spies. Let's go, you two!"

He gave them both a shove, indicating the cellar door.

"Down you go!"

He turned on a light. The switch was on the kitchen wall at the top of the stairs, and Holly hoped they would leave the light on. No such luck! Moore waited until they reached the bottom of the stairs, then slammed the door and switched off the light. They hadn't time to get their bearings before the light was switched off, and the cellar was plunged into darkness.

Holly was scared. Her mother had been right all along. Her curiosity had finally gotten her into trouble, and it didn't look as though she and Tim would be able to get themselves out of this predicament. She had no illusions about the men who had captured them. They were undoubtedly a bad lot, and it was obvious they couldn't afford to let Holly and Tim go. Her anxiety must have been apparent to Tim even in the dark, because he put his arm around her shoulders to comfort her.

"Sit down on the step beside me, Holly. We may be here for a long time," Tim warned, "and the one thing we mustn't do is panic."

"What if they don't let us out, Tim?" Holly's voice was shaking, and she sounded like a little girl. "There aren't any windows down here, and the door looked pretty solid!"

"Well, first of all, we'd better take stock." Tim sounded optimistic. "I have some matches in my pocket. There has to be another light switch down here. That little light at the top of the stairs can't possibly be the only light in this cellar."

Tim fumbled for the matches and found them. He struck one, and the light blinded their eyes. They had become accustomed to the darkness, and the match had burned out before their eyes adjusted. Tim immediately struck another one, and he instructed Holly to start looking for a switch or a pull cord.

They had no sooner begun to look than the match went out, but Tim had seen some old newspapers in a pile. He lit another match and picked up several of them, telling Holly to tear out the pages and twist them into long tapers. They would last longer than the matches, and they would be able to light one off the other.

The men were moving about upstairs, and furniture or something heavy was being dragged across the floor. Tim and Holly didn't have time to think about that now. Their main concern was to find some light.

When they had a good supply of tapers ready, Tim lit two and handed one to Holly. The tapers threw a much better light, so they tucked some of them into their belts. Tim found a light with a pull cord, but the bulb was burned out.

"What are we going to do now?" Holly exclaimed.

"Keep lighting those tapers while I unscrew this bulb," said Tim. "I'll take the bulb out of the socket on the stairs, and if the upstairs switch doesn't control this outlet, we'll at least have some light."

"Super!" Holly exclaimed "Thank goodness you're thinking."

"Well, let's hope it works." Tim was busy as he spoke. He had unscrewed the bulb, and now he was trying to reach the bulb over the stairway, but he was about a foot too short.

"I've got an idea, Holly. If you climb on my shoulders," he suggested, "I'm sure you could reach it. You'll have to grope for it in the dark, so take a good look at your bearings before you climb up. Think you can do it?"

"Sure, no problem," Holly assured him. She was getting some of her courage back at the thought of having some light.

They blew out the tapers, and Tim sat on the stairs while Holly climbed on his shoulders. She groped around till she found the bulb and unscrewed it. Tim helped her down carefully. If they fell on the stairs, they could break a limb, or even worse, the bulb.

Tim lit two more tapers, and they found their way back to the light socket. He screwed in the bulb, and they held their breath as he pulled the string. Light at last! What a glorious luxury!

They took stock of their surroundings. There were some old chairs, a table, old trunks, and dozens of boxes similar to the ones they had found in the cave. Tim looked in the boxes but found them to be empty.

Up to now, Holly and Tim had been too busy to dwell on their immediate peril. They realized there was little more that they could do other than make themselves as comfortable as possible. They had stumbled onto something sinister, and Fryer and his friends couldn't afford to let them go.

"What do you think they'll do with us?" Holly said fearfully.

"I don't know," Tim replied, "but I have a feeling they're too busy to worry about us right now."

"I think I hear a car," said Holly, "but I can't tell if it's coming or going."

"Well, we can't depend on anyone finding us down here," Tim predicted, dismay written all over his face.

Terror

CHAPTER 8

"SHUSH!" TIM WHISPERED. "SOMEONE'S COMING!" HE TOUCHED HIS FINGERS TO his lips and made a wild leap for the light cord, plunging the cellar into darkness again. They clung to each other in terror, not knowing what to expect. Someone was flicking the switch on and off at the top of the stairs.

"Hey, Fryer!" they heard Moore shouting. "The ruddy bulb must have burned out. There's no light in the cellar!"

"Well, use a flashlight or a lantern, stupid!" Fryer yelled back. "We need those boxes down there. Take Dugan with you, and make sure those two little spies don't try anything funny, like attempting to escape or something."

"What are you planning to do with them, Fryer?" Moore questioned. "You can't leave them down there for long. Somebody is going to come looking for them," he cautioned his boss. "Don't forget, the man who owns the store knows they came here."

"You worry too much." Fryer was losing patience with him, and his voice had risen to the shrill shriek of a madman as he thundered at Moore. "Get down there, and get those boxes you lame brain, or I'll lock you up with them. By the time they start looking for those two kids, we'll be miles away from here. Besides," he screamed, "I have plans for them. By the time they are found, they won't be doing any talking."

His voice carried threatening implications, and Tim's protecting arms did little to soothe Holly's trembling little body.

"Oh, Tim," she whispered. "He's going to kill us. We're never going to get out of here." Her voice ended in a tremulous whimper.

Tim patted her shoulder and held her a little tighter to comfort her. He knew from the conversation between the two men that their lives were in great danger. He was just as terrified as Holly, though he tried not to show it.

"Don't be frightened, Holly," he comforted her. "I know it doesn't look good for us at this moment, but I'm sure we'll think of something. Like Moore said, Mr. Duffy knows we came here, and somebody will look for us." Tim was grasping at straws, and he knew it.

"But we told Mr. Duffy we were going to the gypsy camp, so he won't expect us back," Holly reminded him.

"Yeah," he agreed with her, "I forgot about that. We're in a predicament alright, but try not to panic, because if the opportunity to escape arises, we'll have to have our wits about us."

"You're right, of course," Holly acquiesced. "Shush," she whispered. "Here they come."

Moore had obviously found a lantern, and he descended the steps followed closely by Dugan. He made sweeping motions with the lantern until he discovered the corner where Holly and Tim were huddled together.

"So, there you are," he crowed. "I hope your quarters are suitable," he said facetiously. "You may be here for quite a spell, and we wouldn't want you to be uncomfortable, now would we?"

He was obviously enjoying his little joke, but his evil chuckling sent shivers up Holly's spine.

"When are you going to let us out, Sir?" Tim asked hopefully.

This brought loud guffaws from both Moore and Dugan.

"He wants to know when we're going to let them out," Moore said to Dugan gleefully. "And so polite he is. Listen, young fellow, me lad. Take a tip from me. Just don't make a sound, and maybe Fryer will forget you're down here. He's the devil himself, and he'll stop at nothing when he's provoked. Nothing would give him greater pleasure than if you started something, so if you have any ideas about getting out of here, I'd advise you to forget them. Come on, Dugan; help me with these boxes before Fryer takes it on himself to lock us up as well."

The two men began to stack the boxes. Moore had set the lantern on a shelf, and it cast eerie shadows as he and Dugan worked. The light was not bright enough to pierce the darkness of the corner where Holly and Tim crouched in terror. Moore must have felt their fear, because he spun around quickly and hurled one of the boxes in their direction, laughing uproariously as they both ducked to avoid being hit. Fortunately the box just grazed Tim's arm, scratching him slightly.

"Cut it out!" Dugan gritted harshly. "Leave them alone. You've become almost as sadistic as Fryer."

Holly and Tim suddenly felt a spark of hope. Maybe Dugan would intercede for them. They knew it was a slim hope.

"And I suppose you've turned soft in the head," snarled Moore. "Don't forget, you're in this just like Fryer and me. If we get caught because of these two, your hide will burn same as mine."

"Well, stop clowning around," Dugan warned him, "or we'll never get the stuff moved on time."

"What's going on down there?" Fryer was at the top of the stairs yelling his lungs out. "Get a move on, you two," he ordered.

"We're coming," Dugan answered as he picked up a stack of boxes and proceeded up the stairs followed by Moore, who was cursing loudly and complaining about his misfortune in having ever met Dugan. The men made several trips, and soon Holly and Tim were alone again.

They waited until it became apparent that the crooks were finished with the cellar, at least for the time being. Tim searched for the light cord, and again the light brought with it a little comfort. Occasionally, the voices upstairs were raised loud enough to carry, and Holly and Tim were aware that their fate was being discussed in a most frightening manner.

Fryer apparently wanted their disappearance to look like an accident brought on by their own carelessness due to curiosity. He enjoyed plotting and scheming to make a fool of the law, delighting in being the perpetrator of a crime that made no sense whatsoever to the police. His annoyance with Tim and Holly over stumbling into his latest coup only served to prod his most devious imagination.

Holly and Tim heard the words "flood" and "fire" loudly several times in the argument, and their hopes of ever seeing their families again grew more remote with each passing minute. They realized that the only way in or out of the cellar was through the door at the top of the stairs. There wasn't even a coal chute. Tim had already checked for one.

"I can't remember whether I kissed my mom and grandma goodbye or not," Holly said hopelessly. "Wouldn't it be terrible if the last thing they remembered about me was that I was in such a hurry to leave that I never took the time to kiss them goodbye?" Her voice had trailed off into a thin whisper.

"Sure now," said Tim, "you're getting morbid. None of that kind of talk." He was trying to cheer her up. "We'll be fine now, Holly. You'll see. We're a nuisance to Mr. Fryer and his bunch, but they can't afford to waste any time on us. At least we've got to believe that."

His words didn't sound too convincing to his own ears. Suddenly they heard the sound of the key turning in the lock. Tim lunged wildly for the light cord and plunged the cellar into darkness. There was a lot of loud arguing going on at the other side of the cellar door, and Holly and Tim held their breath, terrified at what might be in store for them.

Holly heard herself praying aloud and clamped her hand tightly over her mouth. The terror of the young prisoners was such that they could hear the pounding of their own hearts. The door was suddenly thrown open, and Fryer's voice sent cold chills through them.

"Get down there you two," he yelled, "and get it over with."

Holly gasped. Tim reached for her in the dark. He pulled her down behind some barrels and whispered to her to be quiet. Tim knew they would be found quickly, but he didn't intend to make things easy for the criminals. Dugan was protesting loudly.

"Why don't we just leave them here? They can't get out," he pleaded. "I've never been involved in cold blooded murder before, and they're just a couple of kids."

"Shut up, Dugan. They'll hear you," Fryer hissed. "Now get it done with." He pounded his fist on the wall as he spat out the grim orders.

As Dugan and Moore started down the stairs, there was suddenly a loud knocking at the kitchen door.

"Get back up here, you two," Fryer ordered. Lock the cellar door quickly, and get rid of whoever is hammering on the back door."

Holly and Tim strained to hear, but they couldn't make out what was happening upstairs. For the moment they had been saved by the unknown visitor, but they knew their reprieve would not last long. The voices had quieted down, and Holly and Tim crouched behind the barrels for what seemed like an eternity, waiting for they knew not what.

After an interminable length of time, it occurred to both of them that there was a certain amount of activity going on upstairs. Heavy objects were being dragged across the floor, and the men were shouting orders at each other. It was hard to believe, but for the moment their jailers were apparently too busy to carry out their plan to dispose of them.

Tim pulled Holly to her feet and again reached out for the light cord, bathing them in the comforting glow of the one bulb. They sat and looked at each other, not saying a word, their thoughts going back to the discoveries they had made during the first part of the week.

It had all been such a glorious adventure … just a lark. Was it going to end in this obscure cellar? Holly thought of her friend, Bonnie, in Vancouver. She and Bonnie had grown up together and had shared their innermost secrets. They had done some dangerous sleuthing in the past, poking their amateur detective noses into some of David Brannigan's cases. Their services had been unsolicited by her father, but he agreed they had been able to infiltrate certain areas that would assuredly have been closed to him because of his age.

She wondered what Bonnie was doing now. Was she thinking about Holly and wishing she was spending the holidays with her? Holly was grateful that this was not the case. Bonnie had wanted to come, but her parents had persuaded her to go to Disneyland with them instead. Holly wished she had gone with Bonnie to Disneyland. What a mess she was in!

She thought also of Paul. As far back as she could remember, Paul Castles had been like a big brother to her. He was a year older than

Holly and Bonnie, and the three of them had been inseparable since kindergarten. Paul was like Tim in many ways. He was tall and husky with blond hair, and Holly thought he was the most handsome boy she had ever known. Looking at Tim, she decided that he would stand a close second to Paul, perhaps because she had known Paul all of her young life, and he had managed to rescue her on several rather sticky occasions. Bonnie had always had a crush on Paul, but he had eyes only for Holly, and treated Bonnie more like a pal.

As she looked at Tim, suddenly Holly felt sorry for him. She was the one who attracted danger as bees were attracted to honey. Tim would not be in this situation had it not been for her. No, he wasn't the kind of boy who looked for trouble. He was probably blaming himself for not taking better care of her, but anyone who knew Holly, knew that trouble was her middle name. Anyway, sink or swim, they were in this together.

At this particular moment, some kind of kindred thought passed through their minds, and they simultaneously reached out and grasped each other's hands, squeezing them tightly, as if to give the other strength and comfort.

"I've been wondering who it was that knocked on the back door," Tim said.

"Yes, I've been thinking about that too," Holly told him. "They must have been able to get rid of whoever it was, or maybe it was another one of the gang."

"I hope not. We're in enough trouble with three of them. Let's hope they don't have reinforcements."

Suddenly, it occurred to both of them that the activity upstairs had stopped. There were no voices, and no one was moving about.

"I think they've gone," Tim said softly. "Maybe we can find something to break the door open," he suggested hopefully.

He looked around for an axe or screwdriver, or something they could use as a battering ram, but to no avail.

"Listen! I hear something!" exclaimed Holly.

There was a sound at the door of the cellar. Tim put his arm protectively around Holly and grabbed the light cord again, plunging the cellar into darkness. The door opened, and someone was trying to turn on the light for the stairway.

"Tim and Holly, are you down there?" The voice sounded familiar, but they couldn't place it.

"Yes," Tim answered. "We're here! Who is it?" As he spoke he pulled the light cord.

"Never mind that," the voice answered. "Just come up, and let's get out of here before they come back."

Tim and Holly didn't stop to argue or question further. They were already on their way up the stairs. Anthony Allegro, the gypsy, was cautioning them to hurry quietly. They gratefully obeyed and followed him without a word. He locked the cellar door behind them, explaining that should Fryer and his men come back, they might be duped into thinking that Holly and Tim were still there. Hopefully, it would be some time before they would discover their young prisoners' escape.

Tim's horse was grazing in the field behind the house. He was still hitched to the cart. The black horse was grazing close by.

"Follow me," said Anthony, "and we'll talk. But we must get away from the house quickly."

Tim and Holly were only too happy to comply. They had plenty of questions, but they would have to wait. They followed him gratefully into the woods. The black horse barely touched the ground. *What a beautiful animal,* thought Holly.

No one spoke during the ride to the gypsy camp. It never occurred to Holly and Tim to mistrust the gypsy. They were out of the clutches of those awful men, and, at the moment, Anthony Allegro was a knight in shining armour.

Holly didn't like to think of what might have happened to them if Anthony had not come along, and she wondered just how he knew of their abduction. Whatever the answer, he was a welcome sight. She also wondered how long it would take for Fryer and his men to discover their escape, and if they would take the trouble to come looking for them. She breathed a sigh of relief when they were deep within the dense, wooded area.

The Reunion

CHAPTER 9

CORA MCCLURE HAD APPROACHED THE GYPSY CAMP WITH A GREAT DEAL OF apprehension. If her suspicions were proved to be wrong, she would feel like a complete fool. She hadn't even told Tom what she had in mind for fear he would try to talk her out of what she was about to do. As she walked into the little clearing, one of the women approached her.

"Good day to you, Ma'am. Would you like to have your fortune told? Or perhaps you would like to buy some of our handmade wares?" She pointed to the beautiful woven baskets, tea cozies, and embroidered linens as she spoke.

"Perhaps I will later," Cora said. "But I would like to talk to Mrs. Allegro, if I may."

"Oh, do you know the princess?" the gypsy asked.

"I'm not sure, but I believe she may be an old and very dear friend from many years ago. Is she here?" Cora asked.

"If you will wait here, Ma'am, I will ask if she will see you. What name will I say?"

"Just Cora. Tell her Cora is here."

The gypsy looked at her with a strange expression before she turned towards the largest caravan. She knocked on the caravan door and was told to enter. After a moment, the door opened and the gypsy beckoned to Cora. Cora was trembling as she walked up the steps.

"Leave us alone, Madelena," Mrs. Allegro dismissed the gypsy woman. "Come in, my dear old friend," she greeted Cora.

As Cora entered the caravan, Mrs. Allegro embraced her.

"Cora, how wonderful, I would have known you anywhere."

"Oh, My Lady, I thought I would never see you again before I died."

Cora was crying. She had found Lady Carolyn at last. Forty years had turned the hair to silver, and the years were etched in the fine lines around the eyes and mouth, but Cora could only see the young girl she had mothered so many years ago. Lady Carolyn's eyes were misty as she looked at Cora. She saw the straight, proud back, and Cora's eyes, bright as ever, were flooded with tears of joy.

"I was going to get in touch with you tomorrow after Anthony had completed his mission here. It's imperative that we remain anonymous until them. Come sit here, Cora, and I'll make us some tea. I have so much to tell you. I don't know where to begin; so much has happened in forty years, and my life has been very full and exciting."

Lady Carolyn put the kettle on and set out the china cups and saucers while Cora looked around in amazement. No one would ever guess that a lowly caravan could be so luxuriously decorated. Lady Carolyn's feminine touch was apparent in every detail.

"I see you approve of my taste, dear Cora," she observed with some amusement. "It's not a mansion, but it serves my needs."

"I'm sorry, Lady Carolyn," Cora apologized. "I didn't mean to stare, but I can't believe how beautiful your caravan is."

"Yes, it's extremely comfortable, but you must be wondering why I'm living under these circumstances." She poured the tea as she talked. "Have a cake and we'll have a long talk."

The two ladies chatted and told their individual stories, bringing each other up to date on events and happenings of the forty year separation. They were still talking when Anthony and his young adventurers pulled into the camp. Anthony handed the reins of his horse to one of his men and led the way to his mother's caravan. They had the surprise of their lives when they walked in and discovered Cora McClure sitting on the sofa in the little parlour with Mrs. Allegro.

"Oh, I'm sorry, Mother," Anthony apologized, "I didn't know you had a visitor."

"That's quite all right, Anthony. Come in, dear," she invited him. "I want you to meet a very dear friend."

Suddenly, she became aware that Anthony was not alone.

"Why, Holly and Tim," she exclaimed, "how nice to see you again."

"Thank you," said Holly. "I didn't know you were coming here, Mrs. McClure. Did you come to have your fortune told?" she asked.

"No, Holly, I came for a much more important reason—to renew old acquaintances."

Mrs. Allegro took Cora McClure's hand and patted it affectionately.

"Cora came to visit me," she explained. "It's a long story that can't be revealed just yet, but I understand that you and Tim are aware of some of the circumstances."

She motioned to them to sit down and then continued.

"Cora was my nanny and best friend when I was young. She practically raised me all by herself," Mrs. Allegro said softly.

Suddenly, Holly and Tim understood.

"Then, you're Lady Carolyn?" asked Holly.

"That's right, my dear, but you mustn't spread the news just yet, at least until Anthony has completed the work he came here to do."

Holly was puzzled, but nothing would surprise her anymore. Anthony Allegro took Cora McClure's hand and kissed it gently. It reminded Holly of a movie she had seen, except Anthony didn't click his heels together like the guy in the movie every time he kissed a lady's hand.

"I've always wanted to meet you, Mrs. McClure," Anthony said with genuine pleasure. "I know everything about you. Mother speaks of you often and with great affection. Welcome to our humble home."

Anthony's manners were impeccable, and Cora McClure was almost overcome with emotion. She dabbed at her eyes with her handkerchief as they filled with tears of joy for the second time that day.

"I never thought I could ever be this happy. Looking at you, I feel like Master William has come back from the grave."

"Yes, he does bear a striking resemblance to my brother, doesn't he? I've often thought so. He's also just as wild as William was when he rides his horse. Sometimes he frightens me when I recall what happened to poor William."

"As you can see, my mother is a worrier, at least where I am concerned." Anthony's amusement was evident in his twinkling, black eyes.

"Cora has been telling me of your adventures, Holly," said Lady Carolyn. "You must bring Anthony up to date, as he is involved in this case. By the way, how did you happen to come here with Anthony?"

Holly explained what had happened to them and how Anthony had rescued them.

"One thing puzzles me, though," said Holly. "How did you happen to know we were in the house?" she inquired.

"I had the house under surveillance and was watching from the bushes when Moore forced you into the house," Anthony explained.

Holly remembered hearing the twig snapping in the bushes and realized it must have been Anthony.

"I was able to hear most of what was going on in the house, but I was afraid to leave to summon help, fearing something might happen to you while I was gone. When I heard them planning to dispose of you, and Fryer screaming to get it done with, I knocked on the door to distract them."

"What did you say when they came to the door?" Holly asked.

"Well, I knew I couldn't handle three of them by myself, but I was hoping to rattle them enough so that they would decide to get out of there in a hurry. I told them I was a friend of Mr. Brown's, the owner of the house, and that he had asked me to meet him there to discuss contracting some repairs to the house. They said that I had missed Mr. Brown by several minutes and that I should try to catch him. I pretended to leave and then circled back to the bushes at the back of the house. Within a few minutes, I saw them loading up the van, and I knew they were in too much of a hurry to bother with you anymore, so I waited until they left, and then I picked the lock on the back door."

"Wow!" Tim exclaimed. "We sure were lucky you happened to be there."

"I didn't just happen to be there," Anthony told them. "You can be sure you wouldn't have left the house alive if I hadn't rescued you. Those men have no scruples and wouldn't have permitted a young boy and girl to spoil their plans. I can see I'd better tell you about myself and my interest in these criminals."

He pulled a chair out and sat down beside his mother.

"First of all," he began, "my band of gypsies are not what they seem. They are all trained investigators associated with INTERPOL, which is an international police force. We have followed Fryer and his men across Europe, building a case against them that is unbelievable. Our investigators have uncovered a trail of murder, gunrunning, a drug peddling and distribution ring, and many other criminal offences, all organized by Fryer and his gang. Many of his men have been caught and prosecuted, but Fryer has always eluded us, because he has never allowed himself to become too closely involved in any of his business ventures. He is the top man, and his underlings have always done the dirty work while he did the organizing and planning. Now, however, his gang has become so depleted that he has been forced to take part in the actual transactions, and we're ready to close in. Fryer is the one we want. We believe he is doing his business by sea, as we have been unable to catch him with road blocks or seaport and airport surveillance."

"Anthony," Lady Carolyn interrupted him, "I believe Holly and Tim can shed some light on this. Perhaps you could repeat your experiences in the cave," she suggested to them.

Anthony Allegro listened with avid interest while they told their story, beginning with the tour of the castle, their discovery of a prowler, and their ominous find in the cave the following day. Holly told of seeing the three men going into the cave the evening before, and how they had unloaded several boxes for storage in the chamber. She also told him that the village council was holding a meeting that evening to plan their strategy.

"We heard Fryer and his men say they were moving at midnight tonight," Tim said, "so we'll have to move fast if we're to be ready for them."

"My men and I will be at that meeting," said Anthony. "We don't want anything to go wrong, and I'm afraid your Constable Millar is not capable of handling trouble of such magnitude. I know of your father's experience, Holly, and will be grateful for his help. What time is he expected to arrive?"

"He's due on the four o'clock bus," Holly said, and then gasped. "Oh! We forgot to ask your dad to meet him, Tim!"

"That's right!" said Tim. "Oh well, it's only 2:05; we have plenty of time," he assured her.

Holly had noticed the diary on the little table beside Lady Carolyn, and her curiosity prompted her to ask, "Did the diary tell you how to find Lady Carolyn, Mrs. McClure?"

"Yes," said Cora. "Lady Carolyn said that her prince was a gypsy who was in undercover work for the police, and because of his work, she would have to drop out of sight when she married him."

Lady Carolyn smiled. "Yes, my parents would never have understood or given their permission," she explained, "so there was no other way. I'm sorry for the anguish I caused them, and you, my dear Cora. My brother, William, and I knew about the underground passages and chambers between the cave and the castle. We explored them often when we were children. They were our secret hideaway."

There was a faraway look in her eyes as she spoke.

"Anthony was educated at Oxford and has a law degree," she went on. "His father was very proud of him. They worked well together. My husband died a year ago, and I find I am getting a little too old to travel. Perhaps I will stay in Donnymead. Anthony has contacted my cousin, Robert, and he'll be arriving within a few days."

"I'm so happy to hear that you might stay," said Cora. "I've kept your room ready all these years. Somehow, I knew you would return." There were tears in the old lady's eyes as she spoke.

"Well, now," Anthony broke in on the reverie, "there isn't much time left. Holly and Tim, you must keep out of sight," he warned them. "We want Fryer and the others to believe you are still in the cellar. They'll probably be too busy to check, and they have no reason to believe that you could free yourselves. Mrs. McClure, do you think you could drive the cart back to the castle?" he asked.

"Of course I can!" she replied.

"Holly and Tim will lie down in the back, and we'll cover them with a blanket, and you can drive them through the town slowly, so as not to attract attention. Once you are on the Castle Road you'll be safe, but do not allow yourselves to be seen. I'll see Tim's father and explain the situation to him and ask him to meet Mr. Brannigan at the bus. I must talk to my men and make preparations for this evening. You'd better be on your way now," he urged, "and be careful not to attract attention!"

He picked up a large blanket as he spoke, and they said their goodbyes. Mrs. McClure embraced Lady Carolyn and said they would make plans to see each other after the criminals were caught. Holly and Tim made themselves comfortable in the back of the cart. They decided to cover up just before reaching the village, as it was a hot day.

They waved to Anthony and his mother as Mrs. McClure coaxed the horse on its way. As they reached the edge of the village, Holly and Tim peeked out from under the blanket. They could smell smoke and wondered where it was coming from.

"My goodness," Mrs. McClure gasped, "there's a house on fire!"

"It's Mr. Fryer's house!" cried Tim.

The Volunteer Fire Department was doing their best, but the fire was out of control. A wave of horror passed over Holly and Tim as they realized what a close call they'd had. If Anthony Allegro had not rescued them, they would have been burned alive.

"I wonder if Fryer set the fire," said Tim. "Mr. Allegro believed he would try to get rid of us, but I find it hard to believe that he could be so inhumane as to burn us to death."

"Well, we'd better not stop to find out," said Cora McClure anxiously as she urged the horse to a trot. "Cover your heads, children, and stay down," she warned them. "If this Mr. Fryer finds out you're not in the house, you may be in danger, so be careful!"

They stayed under the blanket until they were well up the Castle Road.

"You can take the blanket off now," Mrs. McClure suggested. "It's a bit hot, but stay down in the cart. We don't know where those men are, and if you sit up they could spot you from below."

Holly and Tim were only too happy to obey. They realized how close they'd come to meeting death, and they had no wish to flirt with the possibility of another chance encounter with Fryer and his men. The criminals couldn't be too far away, since they had big plans for this very evening.

When Mrs. McClure pulled up to the castle gates, Tom McClure came out to meet them. Mrs. Brannigan and Susan hurried out when they saw Cora driving the cart. Holly and Tim climbed out, and Cora told them to go quickly into the house.

"What on earth is going on, Cora?" Tom asked his wife.

"Let's all go inside, and we'll tell you," Cora urged them. "We don't want to be seen."

"What have you been up to now, Holly?" her mother cried in alarm.

"Don't get upset, my dear," Mrs. McClure comforted her. "The children are fine, but we have a lot to tell you and Tom. You'd better listen to this, since you're going to be needed this evening."

"I'll put the kettle on and make some tea," said Grandma Brannigan.

She was obviously dying to hear the latest, and tea was always the best medicine to calm the nerves and loosen the tongue. They all followed her into the cottage and gathered around Mary Brannigan's kitchen table.

Holly and Tim told of their encounter with Fryer and their good fortune in being rescued by Anthony Allegro. They then explained how Anthony was involved in the case and how he and his men would be taking part in the attempt to capture the criminals.

Tom and the ladies were so engrossed in the story that they did little else besides nodding their heads. Holly's mother almost fainted when they related the part about the fire, and she had to have a cold cloth to put on her forehead. Holly's grandma just kept on pouring tea and passing cakes. There was always an endless supply of cakes. They were still discussing the day's events when they heard a car pulling up in front of the cottage.

"Oh, David's here at last," Susan Brannigan cried. She rushed outside, followed by the group, to greet her husband. Anthony Allegro had accompanied them. After a joyous welcome, hugs and kisses and a few tears, Anthony was introduced to the ladies. Again Grandma Brannigan poured the tea, and the discussion continued.

"I asked Anthony to come along with us so that he might fill us in on what's been happening," David Brannigan explained. "You two are very fortunate," he said to Tim and Holly. "I don't know if you realize just how fortunate! Pat tells me the fire at Fryer's house was deliberately set. As far as Fryer's bunch is concerned, they believe they've disposed of you."

Susan Brannigan gave a little cry, and her hands flew to her mouth.

"Don't worry, Susan." He put his arm around her. "We'll get those scoundrels. We have a plan. Anthony has to go back with Pat to organize his men. We'll all meet at seven o'clock in the town hall. I'll drive the horse and cart in, and Tom will accompany me."

David was pacing up and down as he spoke.

"Tim had better stay here," he went on. "We don't want him to be seen by Fryer or his men, as they might panic and call the whole caper off. We have to nail them tonight, as there may not be another chance. The cave entrance is still covered by water, so they won't be in the cave now. Tom, you'd better show Anthony and me how to get to the underground passages by going through the castle."

The men hurried after Tom. They stopped only long enough to pick up some lanterns and the keys to the castle.

The Plan

CHAPTER 10

"WE MUST BE VERY QUIET," TOM CAUTIONED THEM. "WE DON'T KNOW FOR SURE that nobody is down there."

He was using the large iron key to open the door leading to the dungeon.

"That's right," agreed David Brannigan. "We know the three men who were at the house could not possibly be here, as the cave entrance has been covered by water since before noon, and we know where they were at noon, but there may be others."

"I've had them under surveillance for several days," said Anthony, "and as far as I know, there are only three of them. They are very clever, and they know that any more men would attract attention in such a small village. But you're right, we must be very quiet. We can't afford to be careless at this stage."

Tom led the way. The trap door moved easily on its hinges, indicating that it had been used often and recently. It was a sobering thought. How long had these criminals been operating under their noses, and why was that man inside the castle prowling around? The men lowered themselves cautiously through the opening and crept stealthily down the steps leading to the passages.

"This is incredible!" David was astonished. "I lived here for twenty-two years and never knew these passages existed."

They reached the chamber without incident. There was no one there, but there were twice as many boxes as there were the previous day.

"Dynamite and guns!" Anthony was checking each box carefully. "There doesn't seem to be any ammunition for the guns. Good! That means they can't use them on us if we trap them in here."

"What about the dynamite?" Pat Gallagher's voice was shaking. "They could bury us all in here if they use it."

"Not if we remove these four boxes of caps and fuses," said David. "We can each carry a box, and Tim can carry the lanterns."

"Now that we've settled that problem," Anthony said, "I'd like Tim to show me how he and Holly reached this chamber from the cave."

"This way, Mr. Allegro." Tim preceded them down the passage. He indicated the passage branching off to his left. "We didn't explore that passage, so we don't know where it leads."

They continued until they came to the cave, and Tim showed them how he and Holly had managed to climb to such a height. It was amazing that the villagers hadn't discovered the passages before this, even though the passage entrance was not visible until one happened to be on the same level.

"Good," Anthony said approvingly. "Now we must hurry. There's work to be done, and plans to be made. Let's go back and remove the boxes of caps and fuses and arrange the other boxes so they won't be missed."

They climbed back up to the passage and hurried to carry out their plan. Each man carried a box while Tim carried the lanterns. Tom locked the dungeon door behind them, and the boxes were hidden in the wine cellar among the wine barrels.

"We must go now," said Anthony. "There isn't much time, and I must organize my gypsies. We'll meet at seven o'clock in the town hall, and by then we'll have prepared our plan."

It was five after six by the time Anthony and Pat had left. That didn't leave them much time before the meeting. They would have to rush. Tom and David grabbed a sandwich and a cup of tea, and then David quickly changed his clothes. He put on a pair of jeans and sneakers and felt more prepared for whatever lay ahead.

Tim and Holly were not too happy at being left out of the excitement, but felt better when David Brannigan promised they would be used as look-outs. He cautioned them to stay out of sight for the time being, and then he and Tom climbed onto the cart and headed for town. It was ten minutes to seven.

When they reached the town hall, the village council members were all there. There were only eight of them—not a very large army. Pat Gallagher was there and told David and Tom that Anthony Allegro and his gypsies would be a little late, as they were all coming in a wagon. They would be covered so as not to attract attention, and only the driver would be seen. Pat opened the side door so that the wagon could be driven into the alley. In this way, the gypsies would not attract attention when they entered the hall.

The council members greeted David and welcomed him home. They had all known him since he was a child and thought of him as a hometown boy who made good. There was a lot of back slapping and good wishes.

"Let's call this meeting to order." Mr. Duffy was hammering the table with the little gavel.

"We're waiting for some friends, Jim," said Pat. "They should be here any minute."

"Who are we waiting for?" Mr. Duffy was impatient. "Everybody's here."

At that moment, Anthony Allegro walked in followed by nine gypsies. They were wearing their 'kerchiefs and earrings, and the effect was startling. Mr. Duffy and Sean McCarthy started to bristle and sputter.

"What's the meaning of this?" Mr. Duffy was almost blue in the face.

Pat Gallagher, Tom, and David stepped forward and shook each of them by the hand. The council members looked back and forth at each other in astonishment.

"Thank you all for coming," said Pat. "Now if I can have your attention, folks, I will explain these unusual proceedings to you. Everyone have a seat, and I'll introduce our friends here. The council members were all so flabbergasted that they sat down without a word.

"Now folks," Pat began, "you all know David Brannigan," he indicated David as he spoke, "so there's no need to do more than say, 'glad to have you with us, David.'"

There was a ripple of applause and a few mumblings of "here, here."

"But," Pat continued, "you haven't met Mr. Anthony Allegro and his men." He pointed to Anthony as he spoke.

"Mr. Allegro and his gypsies are all trained investigators," Pat explained. "They work for INTERPOL, an organization I'm sure you've all heard of."

The council members all looked unconvinced.

"There has been criminal activity going on in the village of Donnymead that none of us have been aware of."

A murmur went around the room, and now Pat had the attention of every man present.

"My son, Tim, and David's daughter, Holly, happened to stumble on it and almost got themselves killed. If Mr. Allegro hadn't rescued them, they would have been burned up in that fire today. The fire was deliberately set in an effort to get rid of them because they had uncovered something that would terrify every man, woman, and child in this village. Now you know that we're dealing with murderers and arsonists. These are people who will stop at nothing!" Pat banged his fist on the table.

"Anthony Allegro and his men have been following the criminals," he continued, "and we're hoping to combine forces with him and his men to lay a trap for the blackguards. I'm going to ask Mr. Anthony Allegro to come up here and bring you up to date on what has happened so far and discuss whatever plan he has come up with."

There was a sudden burst of applause from the shocked council members, and Anthony Allegro made his way up to the front of the hall. He thanked them for their attention and then explained the situation as it now stood. As he spoke in a quiet, articulate voice, not one man moved or protested.

He was obviously well educated and accustomed to command, and since no one else was qualified in their little village, they were happy to let him handle the situation. Constable Millar looked sick when he realized how inadequate his qualifications were for something of this nature. No one asked his opinion, and he was glad. He wouldn't have known what to do, anyway. He didn't even own a gun.

Anthony Allegro was asking a question.

"How many of you own rifles or hunting knives?"

There was a show of hands. Four had rifles. The others said they would bring knives or clubs.

"If there are any of you who would rather not take part for any reason, please let us know now," said Anthony.

Mr. Duffy stood up as tall as his five foot, seven inches would permit and stuck his chest out.

"I guarantee there isn't a coward in this group, Mr. Allegro," and his eyes bored through Constable Millar. "We're all with you to the last man."

"Aye, aye," came the response from the others.

"Very well then," Anthony acknowledged. "We must do this as quietly as possible. We don't want to alarm the villagers. I believe we can handle it with two teams. David Brannigan will lead one team, and I the other. We'll all meet at the castle. Holly and Tim will be the look-outs. They'll watch for the crooks' arrival at the cave and will signal us when they're inside. Mr. Brannigan's team will go in through the castle, and my men will go down the cliff on ropes and enter the cave once they are sure that the criminals have had time to reach the passage."

Every man in the room strained forward to listen.

"We'll keep a reserve team of four men," Anthony went on. "I expect there'll be a large boat arriving to pick up the shipment. They'll probably lower a small boat, as they will not want to bring the bigger boat too close to the rocks. My four men will go down the cliff and enter the cave, preventing their escape. I'll alert the coast guard by telephone before we leave for the castle and ask them to stand by to arrest the crew of the larger boat. Now, are there any questions?" he asked.

"How are we all going to get to the castle without being detected?" one of the council members asked.

"My men will all ride in the wagon," he replied. "Pat tells me he has a lorry. Three can ride in the front, the rest in the back. Only the driver should be seen, so the rest will have to stay down and out of sight. There will be blankets in the lorry to cover yourselves. You'll be uncomfortable, but the less activity on Castle Road, the better. If there are no more questions, we'd better disperse. I'll phone the coastguard, and you'll procure your weapons. My men and I will leave immediately. You'll come back here as quickly as possible and climb into the truck. Oh, and if you have any flashlights, bring them along. They'll be easier to handle than lanterns, should there be a fight."

Anthony and the gypsies left as quickly and silently as they came. When Pat Gallagher and J.P. Duffy walked by the telephone booth, they saw Anthony Allegro making his phone call. Two horses were hitched to the wagon, but there was no sign of any of the men. The wagon looked as though it was loaded with supplies, and attracted no attention whatsoever.

Tom and David waited in the hall for the men to return. Sean McCarthy and Phil Rafferty both returned with their two burly sons in tow. They would certainly be welcome in case of a fight. Their fathers warned them that they would have to take orders from David Brannigan, and they would be briefed on the way to the castle.

Within fifteen minutes, they were on their way. Pat was driving, and anyone passing on the street would have thought he was the only one in the truck. The men stayed out of sight until they pulled up in front of the castle. Anthony Allegro had just arrived, and his men were climbing out of the wagon.

Tom led them around to the courtyard at the back of the castle so that everyone would be out of sight while Anthony drove his wagon across the bridge and left it inside the courtyard. Now the only vehicle to be seen was Pat's lorry, which was not unusual, as he was a regular visitor at the castle.

Tim and Holly joined the men and they were briefed on their part in the plan. Since it would be dark soon, they would not be seen from below as long as they lay close to the ground, and they would set up watch from ten o'clock to zero hour … whatever time that happened to be.

When Fryer and his men were spotted, they were to crawl quietly away from the edge of the cliff, and Holly would alert the gypsies concealed in the trees behind them. Tim would run around to the back of the castle and alert David Brannigan.

After the gypsies were in the cave, Holly and Tim would watch for the boat and signal the reserve team if a boat was lowered. The gypsies had ropes with special hooks on them, the same as mountain climbers used. They all had knives in sheaths attached to their belts, and they each had a gun in a shoulder holster.

Anthony Allegro had taken off his jacket; he was similarly armed. It was all so exciting. Holly felt as though she was in a movie. Cora McClure had joined her mother and grandmother, and they drank endless cups of tea to calm them. Kevin McCarthy and Wilf Rafferty had been briefed and were flexing their muscles, looking forward to the fray. It wasn't often their little village gave them the chance to prove they were men.

At ten o'clock Holly and Tim took their posts at the point. There was no moon to brighten up the night, and the darkness had come on them very quickly. They settled down for a long wait.

Guilty by Association

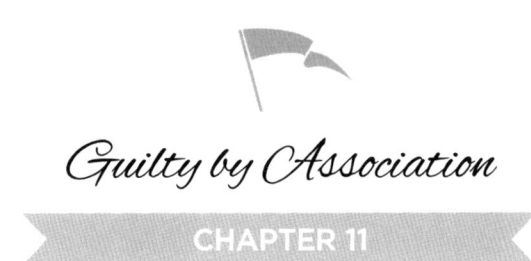

CHAPTER 11

GLEN FRYER PACED BACK AND FORTH LIKE A CAGED CAT. DUGAN AND MOORE watched him nervously. It was dark now, and the light from the lantern wasn't much better than candle light in the huge abandoned barn. Dugan was feeling sick as he remembered how Fryer had set the house ablaze this afternoon. He had protested violently as Fryer poured petrol all through the inside of the house, and just before throwing a match on it, he had tossed a lit lantern down the cellar steps and locked the door again.

The lantern had burst into flames immediately, and Dugan had tried to open the cellar door, only to be zonked on the head by Fryer. The bottle Fryer had used to hit him had broken into little pieces. He could still hear Fryer laughing hysterically as he threw the match on the petrol and ran quickly to the van. Dugan had been so dazed that he had to be half dragged to the van by Moore. Fryer would have left him there to burn along with the kids.

As they pulled out of the village, they heard the siren calling the volunteer fire department out. The house was already blazing, and Dugan knew the two kids were doomed, because no one would expect them to be in the basement.

He had never meant to get into anything like this, and now he was an accessory to murder. Moore didn't seem to be disturbed by the fire or the fate of the young girl and boy. Only Fryer could make him nervous. The boss was an animal devoid of human feelings, and Moore was his chattel. Fryer owned him—hook, line, and sinker.

Moore was like a faithful dog trained to kill on command, and Dugan wondered how he got that way. Both Fryer and Moore had dismissed any thought of the macabre murder of the boy and girl from their minds, but Dugan was haunted by visions of the kids running through the fire, their hair and clothes aflame, screaming and pounding on the door until they succumbed in a pathetic black heap.

Thinking about it started his stomach retching again. Dugan was just a petty thief and swindler, who until now had lived by his wits. He had been recruited by one of Fryer's men when he was down on his luck, and was told that the job was a piece of cake. "Just moving some stolen contraband," he was told.

If they ran into trouble, he would not back down from a good fight and could handle himself with the best of them. But murdering women and children was not his style, and he realized that even though he had tried to prevent it, he was as involved as Moore and Fryer and, in the eyes of the law, just as guilty. He could feel the rope tightening around his neck.

There were a few more boxes in the van, and Dugan was hoping that the pick-up boat would be a large one so they wouldn't have to make too many trips to the ship He wanted to get this over and done with so he could rid himself of Fryer and Moore forever.

Fryer knew Dugan was feeling sick and thought it a huge joke. He kept trying to coax the unhappy man to eat, even though he knew that by just waving a piece of chicken under Dugan's nose he was making him retch. His sadistic sense of humour was frightening, and Dugan knew he was insane.

Fryer paced the floor, chewing on a chicken leg. He and Moore had eaten almost all of the chicken, and they were now becoming impatient. Fryer squinted as he tried to see his watch.

"Okay, you two, it's time to go," he ordered. "By the time we unload this stuff into the boat, it'll be close to eleven o'clock. Moore, you drive—and take it easy. The road is bad, and we don't want any breakdowns on the way. Get a move on, Dugan," he barked. "You're like an old woman."

Dugan didn't have the heart left for the rest of this caper, but he knew he couldn't back out now. Fryer would kill him if he tried to do so. This was small potatoes compared to some of Fryer's deals, but his manpower was depleted, and he had taken so many foolish chances in the past that the underworld found him to be a large risk, and he was finding it more difficult to recruit newcomers into his gang. The word was out that he was poison, like a cobra. He would throw his men to the wolves to save his own skin.

The road into town was full of pot holes, and Dugan thought about the two boxes of grenades in the van and wondered if they were as safe as Fryer had said they were. He was perspiring heavily by the time they reached the road to the pier. It was a dark night. Dugan remembered something his mother used to say when he was young: "Men love darkness rather than light because their deeds are evil."

He wasn't sure where she got it from. Maybe it was the Bible. She was always reading the Bible and quoting from it. Poor old mom. If she could see him now, she would turn over in her grave. He had given her nothing but grief in her lifetime, but she had always stuck by him when he was in trouble with the law and had never given up hope that he would change.

They reached the pier without meeting anyone. Dugan half expected a lynch party to be out looking for them, and was surprised that the town was seemingly asleep. A few lights twinkled from the cottage windows, but most of the windows were dark. People in Donnymead retired early.

It didn't take them long to unload the van, and Moore parked it away from the pier and off the road where it was sheltered by some trees and wouldn't be likely to attract attention.

The boat was low in the water from the weight of the three men and the six boxes of arms. It was slow moving as they started toward the cave. The castle was barely visible against the night skyline.

Dugan's brain was screaming. *How could the whole world be asleep? Didn't they know that murder had been done today?*

Success

CHAPTER 12

"IT'S ELEVEN THIRTY, TIM," HOLLY WHISPERED. "MAYBE WE MADE A MISTAKE, OR maybe they're on to us."

"Maybe," said Tim. "It sure is dark. I bet they picked tonight because there isn't any moon."

"There isn't even one star out," whispered Holly. "Shush! What was that? I think I hear something."

"Yeah," Tim was whispering now. "Don't make a sound."

They listened and heard the sound of oars. They strained to see. They could barely make out the outline of a small boat just below them. In the darkness, they couldn't be sure how many men there were, but the boat was heading into the cave.

Holly and Tim started crawling away from the cliff on their stomachs. When they were clear of the edge, they crouched down and ran—Holly toward the trees, and Tim around the castle. They never said a word. They just touched their fingers to their lips and then pointed, indicating that the boat was in the cave.

It was incredible how quickly the gypsies moved through the grass, crawling like snakes on their stomachs. They had previously left three ropes in readiness at the edge of the cliff, the hooks already positioned deep in the rocks. They waited silently for several minutes to give Fryer and his men time to reach the passageway, and then without a sound they went over the edge three at a time.

Anthony Allegro was one of the first to make the descent. When they disappeared inside the cave, three more followed. The other four waited as prearranged for any sign of another small boat. There was no sound from below. Holly pulled the ropes up and flattened herself to the ground. She thought she heard a muffled shout from the cave then all was quiet.

Tim crawled back silently beside her, indicating that he had fulfilled his duty, and the men were on their way down to the dungeons. They took up their vigil again and watched for another small boat. It was impossible to see if there was a large boat further out, especially since their lights would probably not be on.

When they were level with the cave, Anthony and his men were able to swing themselves onto a ledge. They were agile as monkeys and made no sound as they scrambled from ledge to ledge. They moved so silently that Anthony was on the man who had been left to guard the passage before he knew what happened. Anthony rapped him behind the ear with his gun, but not before the crook managed an attempted warning shout, which was muffled somewhat by Anthony's hand clamped tightly over his mouth.

Someone was coming, and the gypsies crouched in readiness.

"What's the matter, Moore? You're supposed to be quiet. Moore? Answer me, Moore!"

Just then he realized something was wrong and turned to run.

"Fryer," Dugan was running and shouting, "somebody's here."

"Shut up, you fool," Fryer growled. "It's probably the other boat. Where's Moore?"

"That what I'm trying to tell you. Moore doesn't answer me. Something's happened to him."

Just then he spotted Anthony and his gypsies.

"Run, Fryer," he yelled. "We're trapped."

Anthony Allegro and his men were right behind him.

"Follow me, Dugan!" Fryer shouted.

Anthony shone a powerful flashlight down the passage, and suddenly a shot ricocheted down the rock walls, glancing off one gypsy's shoulder.

"I think I got one, Dugan!" Fryer shouted. "Let's get out of here! We'll go up through the castle."

Two more shots rang out, but no one was hit. Suddenly, there was a scuffle up ahead, and David Brannigan's voice came out of the darkness.

"We have one here, Anthony. The other one is headed back in your direction."

They met without intercepting the fugitive.

"He must have slipped down the other passage," Tom McClure predicted.

Turn all your flashlights on, and find the other passage quickly," Anthony instructed.

Someone shone his flashlight into the chamber as they were passing, and suddenly a figure was seen darting behind the boxes.

"He went back in here," shouted young Wilf Rafferty, and he lunged in the direction of the boxes. A shot rang out, and he gave a yell as he clutched his side.

"He got me, Pop," moaned Wilf.

There was a wild roar, and Phil Rafferty charged like a bull into the corner where Fryer was hiding. Three burly Irishmen and several gypsies piled on top of the cowering Fryer, but not before he got out another shot. Anthony Allegro fell to the ground beside Wilf Rafferty.

It wasn't difficult to subdue Fryer after Phil Rafferty got finished with him. He was meek as a lamb when David Brannigan tied his hands behind his back. The gypsies were kneeling beside Anthony and Wilf Rafferty, shining their flashlights on the wounds.

Anthony was unconscious, and his face was covered with blood. Young Wilf Rafferty, on the other hand, was conscious and holding his side.

"Tony! Tony!" A voice echoed down the corridor.

"In here," one of the gypsies answered. "Is that you, Carlos?"

"Yes. Where's Tony?"

A couple of gypsies from the reserve team entered the chamber.

"Tony's been hit. I don't know how bad it is. He's unconscious."

"Let me see," said Carlos.

He knelt down beside Anthony and inspected the wound.

"It's only a surface wound," Carlos assured them. "It looks worse than it is because of the blood. He'll be alright. Look, he's coming around now. Hey, take it easy, Tony."

"What happened?" Anthony asked as he felt his head and tried to sit up.

"It's not so bad, Tony," Carlos affirmed. "The bullet grazed your temple and knocked you out. A few stitches and you'll be fine. The boy here needs medical aid. Do any of you know if there's a doctor in the area? He should go to a hospital."

"There's a doctor in Donnymead, and we have a small nursing home," said Pat Gallagher.

Carlos helped Anthony to his feet and steadied him when he swayed a little.

"Will you be able to walk, Tony?" he asked.

"I'll be fine. Take care of the boy here. He'll have to be carried out of here."

"Do you have anything we could use to make a litter or stretcher?" David Brannigan asked Tom. "He really shouldn't be moved, but the doctor can't work on him down here in the dark."

"I'll find something," Tom said. "I think I know where there are some old doors. Would that do?"

"That would be great," said David.

"I'll be right back then."

Anthony Allegro suddenly realized that his reserve team members were all in the chamber.

"What are you doing here, Carlos?" he asked.

"We got them all, Tony," Carlos explained. "There are two more down in the cave, and they won't be moving for a long time. I saw the coast guard boat pull up beside their boat, and I signaled to them that we had everything under control at this end. Dominique got a flesh would in the shoulder, but it's not too bad," he assured Anthony.

Tom was back in a few minutes with an old door.

"It won't be too comfortable," said Tom, "but it's all I can find."

"It'll work fine," said David. "Put it down beside Wilf, and we'll lift him onto it. We'll try not to hurt you, Wilf," he said to the boy.

"Don't worry, Mr. Brannigan. Just get me out of here."

Wilf was trying to put on a brave front, but when his father and two others lifted him and slid him onto the door, he groaned loudly.

"Sorry, Wilf," David comforted him, "but we have to get you to a doctor as quickly as possible."

The men picked up the makeshift stretcher, and it was a strange procession that made its way up through the dungeons into the castle. Fryer had finally met his match, and when he saw Holly and Tim very much alive, he looked as though he was seeing a couple of ghosts. His face turned white, and he almost fainted.

Phil Rafferty kept telling Fryer he hoped he would blink even an eyelash, as nothing would give him more pleasure than to use the club he was carrying to make an impression. It was obvious that Fryer wouldn't give him the opportunity to carry out his threat, much to Phil Rafferty's frustration.

David called the village doctor and an ambulance to transport young Wilf Rafferty to Belfast General Hospital. The ladies bustled around Wilf and the two wounded gypsies, trying to make them more comfortable until the doctor arrived.

Constable Miller was strutting around the subdued criminals. The fact that they were tied up, of course, tended to give him added courage. It had been years since the village of Donnymead had seen such goings on. There was only one small cell in the police station, which rarely held anything more criminal than Johnny Gillis, the village drunk. Johnny was harmless—just a little noisy on a Saturday night.

Doctor Brady arrived within a very few minutes. He tended to Wilf first.

"Well now, young fellow," he teased him. "It looks like you're going to be flirting with the pretty nurses for a week or two."

"Then I'm not going to die?" asked Wilf.

"Not this time, Wilf," the doctor promised. "It doesn't look as though the bullet has hit any vital organs, but we can't tell much till we get you to a hospital and remove it. I promise you one thing, though. You won't die."

"The ambulance is on its way, Doctor Brady," David assured him.

Doctor Brady sterilized the wound and covered it with gauze. Then he attended to Anthony and Dominique. Their wounds, though not serious, both required stitches. For a while, Cora McClure's kitchen looked like a hospital room.

The ambulance finally arrived, its siren shattering the early morning stillness of Donnymead. Wilf Rafferty was carefully lifted onto a stretcher and bundled inside, his father climbing in beside him. Once more, Phil Rafferty shook his fist menacingly in the direction of Fryer and his men before the attendants closed the ambulance doors on him. Doctor Brady cautioned Anthony and Dominique against overexertion and told them to drop in and see him in a few days. Then he climbed into his car and followed the ambulance.

Anthony asked Cora if he might use her phone to call the coast guard.

"Of course you may, my dear," she said as she pointed to the phone.

She was feeling quite motherly towards him. After all, wasn't he Lady Carolyn's son?

The gypsies were helping to load the criminals into the back of Pat Gallagher's lorry, and they stood guard with their guns drawn while waiting for Anthony to complete his calls.

After calling the coastguard, he put in a call to the Belfast City Police and asked them to send a black maria (the Irish version of the paddy wagon). Meanwhile, Fryer's gang would have to share the small cell at Constable Millar's gaol with the two men captured from the boat. He next put in a call to INTERPOL and made his report. When he had hung up the phone, he called Holly and Tim over.

"I want to thank you both for your part in helping us to capture Fryer. If you hadn't discovered the passages and chamber where they were storing their contraband, they might very well have gotten away tonight. We are very grateful to you both, and you'll receive a reward for aiding in their capture."

"Thank you, Mr. Allegro, but the reward isn't necessary. We were happy to do what we could. Isn't that right, Tim?" she said.

"That's right, Mr. Allegro," Tim agreed.

"Nevertheless, you will receive a reward and a special commendation," he insisted.

"Who were they selling the weapons to?" Holly inquired.

"As you know, Northern Ireland is a strife torn country due to the differences that are both political and religious. The British government has sent troops in to try and keep peace, but the outlawed Irish Republican Army manages to keep trouble stirred up and the cauldron boiling." Anthony paused and chose his words carefully.

"The weapons you discovered," he went on, "were being sold to the I.R.A. and would have been used against the British Army or business and industry in Northern Ireland. Fortunately, Donnymead is one of the few villages in Northern Ireland that has been untouched by these tragic events, and up to now has escaped the violence. Fryer doesn't care who he does business with. He has been known to sell weapons to both sides in a revolution. Hopefully, he will be out of circulation for a long time. It's scum like him that manages to profit from the misery and suffering of others."

Anthony said goodbye to the ladies and promised Cora that he would bring his mother to see her tomorrow. Then he shook hands with Tom and David and thanked them for their help.

"It's a pleasure to know you, Anthony," said David Brannigan. "I wish I had you and your gypsies working with me in Canada."

"Please call me Tony," he said. "Only my mother calls me Anthony."

He called out to his men. "We'd better go now. It's going to be a little crowded on the return trip, so take care to guard the prisoners well," he warned them.

It was almost five o'clock in the morning when they all pulled away from the castle. Holly didn't believe she would be able to sleep after all the excitement.

Her grandmother chased her off to bed as soon as they reached the cottage, and her dreams that night were reminiscent of a Disney movie, with gypsies dangling from the cliffs while violins played, and gypsy ladies in gaily coloured dresses and kerchiefs danced under a starlit sky around an open fire.

Home Sweet Castle

CHAPTER 13

HOLLY SLEPT UNTIL NOON. HER GRANDMA HAD BEEN UP SINCE NINE O'CLOCK, but had not disturbed Holly or her parents. She was still tired, even though she had slept well. When she went downstairs, her mother and father had just finished breakfast.

"You just missed Tim, Holly," her grandma told her. "He was late today, but he said he would be back later on this afternoon. Anthony Allegro is bringing his mother out to see Cora, and Tim will be driving them, as Pat's going to be busy. I wonder why she's coming to see Cora?" she mused.

"Oh!" Holly exclaimed. "In all the excitement, I forgot to tell you. You'll never believe it, Grandma. Are you ready for this?"

"Well, go on, child," her grandmother urged. "Out with it. What did you forget to tell us?"

Holly was obviously enjoying her grandmother's impatience.

"Lady Carolyn and Mrs. Allegro are one and the same," she burst out with the news.

"Bless me soul," her grandma gasped. "Are you sure, child?"

"Positive," Holly went on eagerly. "Mrs. McClure was at the gypsy camp yesterday. She had discovered when she read the diary that Mrs. Allegro and Lady Carolyn are the same person."

Her parents and grandma were shocked. Holly told them the whole story.

"Oh my," her grandmother said. "I wonder what Sir Robert will say when he hears the news. He's due here today or tomorrow, Cora told me."

"That's why he's coming," Holly explained. "He already knows. Mr. Allegro has contacted him, and Lady Carolyn may be staying at the castle after she talks to Sir Robert."

"Well, that's good news," said David. "Mrs. McClure must be very happy!"

"Yes, she certainly is," Holly agreed.

"Holly," her mother said with a worried look on her face, "please promise me you'll stay out of trouble today."

"I promise, Mom," she said cheerfully.

"What are you planning to do?" her mother asked cautiously, almost afraid of the answer.

"I'm going to write another letter to Bonnie and tell her everything that's happened. By that time, Tim should be here."

Her mother sighed resignedly, and Holly heard her father chuckle as she went to her room. She looked for a pen and writing pad, and then decided since it was such a lovely day, she would write her letter in the garden.

She was still a little groggy from her previous evening's escapades. Her grandma gave her a blanket to spread on the ground, and she sprawled across it and began her letter. How she wished Bonnie was here. Too bad she had missed all the excitement. Bonnie would have loved every minute of it.

Holly had written four pages and decided it would take a book to tell her friend everything that had happened. She closed her eyes just for a moment to concentrate and was suddenly aware that someone was shaking her. She had been sleeping.

"Holly! Wake up! It's me!"

Tim's voice seemed to come from a great distance away.

"Oh, Tim," Holly sat up and rubbed her eyes, "I must've dosed off. What time is it?" she asked.

"It's ten past four," Tim announced. "You've been sleeping the day away."

"Oh, I've slept for almost three hours," Holly cried. "Where are Lady Carolyn and Mr. Allegro?"

"They're talking to your pop. Let's go," Tim urged. "Hey," he exclaimed. "Somebody else is coming. It's Sir Robert. We'd better tell Lady Carolyn."

They ran into the cottage with the news, and everyone came out to meet the car. The door opened, and a handsome, elderly gentleman stepped out.

"Well, well!" he greeted them. "What have we here, Mary? Are you having a family reunion?"

Cora and Tom McClure were coming through the bridge and hurried to greet him.

"Sir Robert, Mary Brannigan said, "it's grand to have you home again. Yes, my family is visiting me. You know my son, David, and this is his wife, Susan and my granddaughter, Holly."

"How do you do, I'm very pleased to meet you." He shook each of them by the hand and welcomed them to Donnymead.

"And Cora! How are you? And Tom!"

Suddenly, he noticed that Cora was close to tears.

"What's wrong, Cora? Do I see tears?"

"Oh yes, Sir Robert, tears of joy." She was obviously overcome with the news. "Sir Robert, may I present Lady Carolyn and her son, Anthony!"

"Carolyn!" Sir Robert took both her hands. "Oh, my dear cousin, so many years! We were just teenagers when I saw you last."

He put both arms around her and embraced her.

"How wonderful, my dear, that you are home at last. And Anthony!" He looked for a moment at Anthony's face as he gripped his hand in a warm handclasp.

"Yes, I can see the resemblance to William, your mother's brother. You must forgive my emotion," he said. "This has all come as quite a shock to me … a pleasant one, I might add. Cora, we must celebrate. I would like to talk to Lady Carolyn and Anthony alone. They must tell me all about themselves. Would you please make us some tea, and serve it in the drawing room?"

"Certainly, Sir Robert," Cora replied happily. "I will see to it immediately."

"Then in one hour from now," Sir Robert said, "I would like all of you to join us, and we will drink champagne to welcome Lady Carolyn and Anthony back to their home."

"I heard you were coming, Sir Robert," said Cora, "and I prepared your suite this morning. I'll call the staff right away."

"Thank you, Cora. You're a treasure," he flattered her. "Shall we go and have our tea?"

He ushered Lady Carolyn and Anthony along the walk.

Holly and her family watched them go, and there were tears in her mother's and grandma's eyes.

"I have some more good news," said Tim. "Casey's Aunt arrived today and gave Mr. Duffy permission to keep Casey. Casey was doing cartwheels when I left."

"Oh, that's wonderful," cried Holly. "This is the best vacation I ever had," she enthused.

"Yes," her mother sighed, "and not even a week has gone by. How can I ever endure another five weeks of worrying about you?"

"Relax, Susan." Her husband was laughing. "You worry too much."

Holly threw her arms around her mother and kissed her.

"Poor Mom," she comforted her. "What will you do when I become a lawyer?"

"I'll probably die a thousand deaths," she groaned.

Toast to a Lady Gypsy

CHAPTER 14

"MY COUSIN, LADY CAROLYN, HAS CONSENTED TO STAY IN DONNYMEAD AS Mistress of this lovely old castle." Sir Robert seemed genuinely pleased.

"Will you please stand and raise your glasses with me in a toast of welcome to my lovely cousin."

Everyone in the room stood up and touched glasses.

"To Lady Carolyn," the toast echoed around the lovely, spacious old drawing room.

When everyone was seated again, Anthony stood up and placed his arm around his mother's shoulder affectionately.

"I should like to answer that toast for my mother, if I may," he said to Sir Robert. "First of all, I would like to thank you for the words of welcome, Cousin Robert. You can't possibly know what that means to my mother and me, especially to mother." Anthony paused and patted his mother on the shoulder. Then he continued.

"Donnymead Castle has always been very dear to my mother's heart. She chose our lifestyle because of her love for my father. He was a very dynamic man with many talents. Till the day he died, he worshipped the ground mother walked on."

Lady Carolyn's eyes were misty as she listened to her son's speech.

She was extremely proud of Anthony, who had loved his father dearly and had felt the loss as much as she when he had died.

"Mother was always Lady Carolyn to my father," he went on. The gypsies idolized her and called her 'Princess.' She was held in high esteem by all of them. Mother saw to it that I was educated. I went to all the best schools and was properly steeped in the cultures of our heritage, but I have never been ashamed of my humble caravan home, because my parents instilled pride in me, a very necessary quality in any self respecting gypsy."

Anthony paused again momentarily and looked at Sir Robert as he continued.

"The gypsy way of life is not easy, but my work requires that I continue to live as a gypsy. Mother, however, has reached an age where travelling has become difficult for her, especially now that she has lost the companionship of my beloved father. I would again like to take this opportunity to thank my cousin, Sir Robert, for his kindness in welcoming mother back to her home. Will you join me, please, in offering a toast of thanks to Sir Robert."

Again the glasses were raised.

"To Sir Robert!" The toast was repeated around the room.

Sir Robert rose to his feet in response to the toast, and there was a ripple of applause to encourage a few words from him.

"Thank you, my dear Anthony." Sir Robert was becoming quite merry. "This lovely old castle has not known laughter and merriment since you left, Carolyn my dear. We're going to have a party, a gala affair such as your father, Lord Mead, tossed in the old days. The world is going to know that my lovely cousin is still with us in the land of the living. We shall have to think of a plausible story to explain your disappearance, my dear, so as not to uncover Anthony's valuable work, and everyone here shall be sworn to secrecy."

Sir Robert was really getting carried away with his plotting, and murmurs of agreement prodded him onward.

"This castle and all its holdings are, of course, your inheritance, Anthony. I shall be quite content to visit once or twice a year, if you will permit me. The castle should have permanent residents and not just an occasional visit. I was never quite sure what my reasons were for not selling it, but I'm so glad now that I didn't. My business interests do not leave me the time to care properly for the estate, and I certainly don't need the inheritance. You both have my blessing, Carolyn and Anthony."

"You may come as often as you wish, Robert," said Lady Carolyn. There were tears of happiness welling up in her eyes, and Holly noticed there were a lot of misty eyes in the room.

"The castle is just as I remembered it. It's as though I've never been away. I know it will take time, but I would like to have some of the suites restored, especially mother's and father's suites. There will always be a suite kept in readiness for you, Robert dear, so please feel that this is your home always."

"Thank you, dear cousin. I shall take advantage of your kind offer as often as possible."

Cora left the room to organize the staff. They had arrived several minutes ago, and there was plenty to do. There was an atmosphere of expectancy about them when they were informed of Lady Carolyn's return, and they hurried to expedite their duties quickly in preparation to meeting their new mistress.

Holly and Tim grinned at one another, pleased that they were in part responsible for this happy turn of events.

"Do you still want to explore the other passages in the cave?" Tim asked her.

"Of course I do," Holly said eagerly. "When can we go?" she asked.

"The coastguard removed the guns and dynamite this morning," he told her, "so we can go tomorrow if you like. The coastguard found two more chambers in the other passage, even larger than the first. There wasn't any contraband in them, but he found evidence of them having been used in the past."

"What did he find?" Holly was overcome with excitement.

"Just some old furniture, as though someone had used it for a hideaway at some time."

"Oh super!" Holly exclaimed. "Maybe it was used as a smuggler's lair."

"Holly has been reading too many detective novels." Her father had overheard them talking. "She is an incurable romantic," he told Tim. "I couldn't help overhearing your conversation, and if you don't mind an old man butting in, I would like to come along with you tomorrow."

Holly laughed. "Daddy, you're as much a romantic as me, and you have the soul of an adventurer. Where do you think I inherited it from?"

"Well, certainly not from your mother," her father laughed heartily.

"Better not tell Mom where we're going tomorrow," she teased him. "Mom is smiling for the first time since arriving at Donnymead."

They looked over at her mother. The frightened look was gone, and she was in animated conversation with Lady Carolyn, who wanted to know all about Canada. She said she hoped to visit both Canada and America some day and was immediately extended an invitation to visit the Brannigan's.

Lady Carolyn said she would discuss it with Anthony, and they would arrange a time suitable to both Susan and herself. Susan Brannigan was ecstatic. She had never entertained a real Lady before … at least not one with a title … and she was sure she would be the envy of all her friends. She would have to have the house all redone to suit the occasion and hire a maid for the period of time Lady Carolyn chose to stay. Lady Carolyn must have guessed what was going through the younger woman's mind, and she told her that she mustn't go to any extra trouble or expense if she did decide to visit. After all, her home had been a caravan for most of the forty years that she had been away, and she felt more at home in a family type atmosphere.

Susan, however, was not going to be deprived of her moment of glory. She was an excellent hostess and loved to entertain, and she intended to outdo herself in seeing that she did everything that was proper.

Sir Robert was enthralled with the story of the previous four day's happenings and asked dozens of questions. He also asked to join the party of explorers the following day. Lady Carolyn was the centre of attraction. One by one, the staff was seen peeking around corners to catch a glimpse of her ladyship.

Their curiosity had not gone unnoticed by Lady Carolyn, and she graciously asked to be introduced to them. When Cora went to the kitchen with the request, there was a great flurry of excitement. Uniforms were checked, and hats and aprons tidied in anticipation, each servant hoping to make a good impression.

They needn't have been concerned about Lady Carolyn's reaction to meeting them. They found her to be a warm and lovely lady. She spoke to each of them, asking them questions about their family life and their specific positions of employment and duties at the castle. A lady was not expected to take such an interest in the household staff, and they all loved her.

She asked if they were happy working at the castle and if they would be willing to continue working for her on a full-time basis. They each said they would be proud to serve her and would make immediate arrangements to move into the castle permanently.

Lady Carolyn told them that the servant's quarters would be decorated immediately. Pat Gallagher had promised to hire the painters and plasterers, and she promised that they would be made comfortable as quickly as possible.

Holly was still puzzled by something, and when Lady Carolyn returned to the drawing room, she decided to take the plunge and ask her if she would mind explaining her gift of prophesy.

"Lady Carolyn," Holly had lowered her voice to a half whisper. She didn't want anyone to think her silly.

"Yes, Holly my dear?"

"Well, I hope you don't mind my asking you, but would you tell me how you happened to predict with such accuracy the events that occurred in the last few days. Are you really clairvoyant?"

Lady Carolyn smiled.

"The gypsies believe that I am gifted," she said. "They call it the gift of second sight. I prefer to think of it as a woman's intuition. You see," she went on to explain, "I had information at my disposal that enabled me to put certain assumptions together and reach conclusions. When I first saw you, Holly, I realized how much you resembled the portrait of me as a young girl that hangs in my room. I believed that Cora would be compelled to show it to you. Then I mentioned the box hidden in the fireplace, and I was sure you would mention it to Cora. Knowing of her curiosity, I was sure she would investigate."

She paused for a moment, deep in thought.

"But how could you know that we would find the underground tunnels or passages?" Holly asked.

"That's simple to explain, my dear," Lady Carolyn laughed. "Everyone who comes to Donnymead eventually visits the cave. I was counting on your natural curiosity and felt that you would do more than just take a quick look inside. You reminded me of myself as a young girl, Holly. William and I both had the hearts of adventurers."

"But how did you know that a discovery would be made involving the police?" Holly questioned.

"Well, as you know, I had advance knowledge of Fryer's operations, and I knew that Anthony was about to close in on him and his men. It was a simple matter of deduction. We knew Mr. Fryer was up to something illegal, and since his capture was imminent, the police would be involved. Concerning my prediction that someone would be hurt, that is something that usually occurs in a confrontation between criminals and police. So, you see, my predictions were all logical deductions."

Lady Carolyn's explanation seemed logical, but Holly still wasn't convinced that she wasn't clairvoyant. As she turned to go and find Tim, Holly noticed that Lady Carolyn had a strange smile on her face, as though she knew just what Holly was thinking.

OTHER BOOKS BY KATHLEEN

Scuba Hijinks
ISBN 978-1-4866-0805-8
Scuba Hijinks is the second book in the "Holly Brannigan Mystery" series. Set on the West Coast of Canada in the Lions Bay and Porteau Bay area, the story follows the adventures of teen sleuth Holly Brannigan and her friends, Bonnie, Paul, and Ted as they team up with Holly's father, Detective David Brannigan, to catch a gang of rogue scuba divers. Holly and her friends learn to scuba dive in order to pursue the criminals, and they bravely face challenges and dangers throughout the case. Thrust into a world of kidnapping and vandalism, the amateur detectives use their new skills and unlimited trust in each other to bring the gang to justice.

All Roads Lead to Home
ISBN 978-1-4866-0789-1
Kathleen has discovered something magical in every province of this grand country, Canada. She sees the beauty in God's gifts to us: the mountains, the valleys, the trees, and the rivers and lakes, which have all inspired her poetry. Most poems are spiritual, some are for children, and some area just plain silly. Come and journey through the hills of Ireland, the cities of Ontario, and the majestic mountains of British Columbia with Kathleen's poetry. She hopes you find something to warm your heart.

Kathleen W. Forbes wrote her first poem when she was eight years old. The poems in this collection were written over the course of Kathleen's lifetime, and provide a small glimpse of her journey from childhood to the present day. As she changed over the years, so have her poems. In this way, they reflect the nature of life itself. Kathleen's father, also a poet and a pastor, once told her that he treasured her poems, which was the greatest accolade of all.

Camping at Blueberry Mountain
ISBN 978-1-4866-0797-6
An adventure is afoot in the town of Green Oaks as eight-year-old Penelope Henry gets the best surprise of her summer: a camping trip to beautiful Blueberry Mountain. The whole family, including her mama, papa, and brother Zinger, pack up their cart and head into the wilderness to relax, meet new lifelong friends, and learn valuable lessons that will forever change them.
But not everything about Blueberry Mountain is as peaceful as it seems. When a group of bandits start causing trouble in camp, it's up to Penny and her friends to save the day—with the help of an irreverent leprechaun named Dinty, who only appears to children.

Penelope Henry at the Circus
ISBN 978-1-4866-0793-8
Penelope's world turns upside-down with the arrival of the circus in her normally quiet village of Green Oaks. Just in case that's not exciting enough, it's also her ninth birthday!
When a monkey escapes from the circus and gets into a tangle with one of Penelope's friends, the circus owner invites them all to see the show—for free. All of Penelope's dreams come true when she is chosen to participate in one of the circus's most exciting acts.
But trouble strikes when the lions get out of their enclosure and the elephant trainer mysteriously goes missing, threatening the entire circus. Will the show be able to go on? With the help of Dinty the leprechaun, Penelope and her new friends are sure to have their hands full.

Penelope Henry at the Country Jamboree
ISBN 978-1-4866-1000-6
Country Jamboree will take you on a weekend of fun for the whole family. Join Penelope and her family and friends down on the farm for a rodeo with their country cousins where they'll watch the horse racing, the chuck wagons, and trick riding! Encounter mystery and discovery with surprises around every corner. Although facing danger and uncertainty, Penelope and friends are protected by Dinty Finnigan, the Irish leprechaun who protects small children and brings fun and magic everywhere he goes. Penelope and her friends will guide you on adventures great and small as they explore the farm and all the fun to be had!
Kathleen has been writing since she was a little girl. Growing up in Ireland, she was regaled with the legends woven into the histories of the castles, the Giant's Causeway, the leprechauns, and little people. When her children came along, she wrote lullabies, poems and stories to enchant and entertain them. It was before, television, computers or the electronic devices available today. She hopes that Penelope Henry will entertain beginning readers and adults alike.